Cover Design and Interior Format
© KILLION
THE
GROUP, INC.

HIGHLAND VENGEANCE

1 THE BAND OF COUSINS

KEIRA MONTCLAIR

CHAPTER ONE

Spring 1284, The Highlands of Scotland

A LOUD THUD AND A SOFT whimper carried to Maggie Ramsay across the ravine, causing all her strength and resolve to desert her in an instant.

Her greatest fear had just happened in front of her. Her sister Molly, whom she had always been driven to protect, was hurt, and it wasn't a light sprain or a bruised hip, not after she'd fallen from such a great height. An arrow had come at them, and while it had missed Molly, she'd tumbled down to the bottom of the ravine.

Just before her sister had fallen, Maggie had caught sight of a man in the distance, in the opposite direction of the archer, though he'd disappeared in an instant. She could have sworn he'd had a large bird of prey resting on his shoulder. Had Molly not fallen, she would have followed him, but she made the only decision she could, hurtling across the moss-covered ground of the Highlands to tend her sister.

"Molly?" Maggie whispered, picking her way down the ravine as fast as she could. Molly's husband, Tormod, was right behind her. The two of them had brought Maggie out to teach her the tracking skills they'd learned from spying for the Scottish Crown, a lesson that had excited her, but the arrow had come out of nowhere. It should have been impossible—they knew the area extremely well, and there weren't any obvious signs of interlopers—but there was no denying it had happened.

"What happened?" Tormod demanded, his face bearing all the fear and worry that Maggie herself felt.

"She…she dodged the arrow and she fell." Both of them knew what a fall from such a height could mean. Molly had rolled or bounced a good distance before finally reaching the bottom of the ravine.

They finally reached her, and Maggie had to swallow a gasp. Her sister lay unmoving, though at least she did not appear to be lying in an unnatural position. Perhaps she'd merely been knocked out from the fall.

Maggie bent down, grabbing her dear sister's hand. "Molly? Wake up, please."

Tormod, whose face had lost all color, reached for her cheek. "Molly, come back to me. Do you hear me? Your sister and I need you. Wake up for both of us."

The barest of a whimper came from her, a sound that reached inside Maggie's soul to squeeze every ounce of emotion from her. She'd heard that sound before—it was the same whimper Molly used to make after taking one of the beatings meant for Maggie when they were wee children, back in the time before Clan Ramsay.

Maggie wished to sob openly, but held her feelings in check. *Not now. Keep those thoughts at bay and take care of your sister.*

Molly opened her eyes, confusion in her gaze. "Maggie?"

"Are you hurt, Mol? Tell me where. Tormod and I will get you home safely to Aunt Brenna." Brenna was the renowned Ramsay healer, married to the former laird of their beloved adopted clan. If anyone could make Molly well again, it was their aunt.

Tormod reached for Maggie's hand to silence her. Pointing into the distance, in the direction of the man Maggie had seen, he whispered, "Someone was there, mayhap he fired that arrow toward her. I'll see if I can find him."

It felt desperately important to set him to rights. "I saw him, too. I don't know why he was there, but I didn't see a bow in his hand. The arrow came from a different spot to the north." She pointed, so Tormod changed his direction to pursue the archer. Two strange men on Ramsay land? That was unheard of in their clan. They were usually well protected.

Tormod left to check the area, bow in his hand, and she could only pray he wouldn't be hurt, too.

"What happened?" Molly asked, her eyes fluttering as she tried her best to keep them open.

"Hush. Do not strain yourself. You took a hard fall from the top of the ravine. Can you move your legs? Your arms? We need to see if anything is broken before we move you."

Molly wiggled her feet and her hands. "I think my feet are fine, but my left arm hurts really badly." She suddenly grabbed her sister's arm in a tight grip. "Maggie!" she shouted. The look in her eyes had shifted to sheer horror.

"What? I'm here for you. What is it?"

"I saw something…saw…" Her head fell back, but she forced it up again until their gazes met. "Trouble. Maggie, you must be careful. I saw something dark near you. It was so strong that I didn't notice the archer before 'twas too late. Promise me you'll be careful." She took a deep breath and gasped.

"What exactly did you see, Mol?" Her sister had the rare ability to see what was ahead, something everyone in the clan had learned to heed.

Molly dug her fingers into her arm so tightly that it pained her, causing her to shudder at her next words. "Maggie, beware. Something, someone…" She swallowed hard and let go of her arm. "Nay."

"What is it?" The hair on her arms stood strong—her sister's premonition was too vague to be avoided.

"My ribs," she panted a few breaths, then held the air. "It hurts to…breathe." She closed her eyes and changed her breathing to slow, shallow breaths.

Their brother, Gavin, came running over, his constant

companion and cousin, Gregor, beside him. The two were inseparable and had been since childhood. Though the lads hadn't been out tracking with them, she wasn't surprised to see them. They oft wandered the woods, just as she and Molly and Tormod did.

"What happened?" Gavin asked. "Molly's hurt?" He did a poor job of trying to hide his surprise, shifting his wide-eyed gaze from Gregor to Maggie and back again.

Gregor shook his head. "I can hardly believe it. Molly has the surest feet of anyone."

Maggie knew how he felt. Her sister seemed invincible most of the time. "She dodged an arrow and fell all the way down the ravine. It knocked her out and she may have broken bones. We need a cart to carry her to Aunt Brenna. She'll not be able to walk or ride a horse." She'd not mention Molly's premonition to anyone just yet.

"Who shot at her?" Gregor asked. His gaze scanned the area. The trees were just budding, so it was easy to see in the distance. In the summer, the lush Highland greenery could hide even the largest of men.

"I didn't recognize the man, but Tormod went after him." She pointed in the direction he'd run. "There was another strange man," she added, nodding in the opposite direction, "but he wasn't the archer. He stood a good distance away." She paused to scan the area, making sure they were still safe. Molly had already been hurt, aye, but she could be hurt worse…and so could the rest of them.

"What did he look like?"

"Tall, long hair, I think dark brown, but he was quite a ways yonder, so I didn't get a good look."

"Whose plaid?" Gavin and Gregor continued to pepper her with questions, one voice blending in with the other as she stared at her sister, soothing herself with the sight of Molly's regular breaths. Mayhap she was not all right now, but she would be.

"No colored plaid." She lifted her gaze to the area where

she'd seen him. "He was dressed all in black. Black tunic with a black-and-white plaid. I think he had a bird on his shoulder, mayhap a hawk? He might have been with the shooter." She could feel her voice rising as the panic grew deep inside her belly.

"The man in black wasn't with the shooter." Her brother's conviction caught her attention.

"Nay, he wasn't," Gregor echoed.

Another thought stopped her cold. "Could it have been a falcon? Molly told me about a man called the Wild Falconer. If *he* was with the shooter, we may have a larger problem on our hands."

"Nay," repeated Gavin. "He was not with the shooter."

The two were so emphatic in their denials that she turned to stare at them, waiting for them to explain themselves. When they didn't, she asked, "How could you be so sure?"

"Because we were with him," Gregor said, crossing his arms. "We'll get Molly back. Never mind about him."

———◆———

WILLIAM MACLERIE, OR WILL AS he preferred, paused for a moment after he saw the arrow swish through the forest toward the Ramsay girl. As soon as the other girl, Maggie, ran down to help her, he took off into forest, bent on catching the man who'd fired the arrow. He'd noticed the strange one off in the distance after he left Gavin and Gregor, but he hadn't expected him to attack the Ramsays. His feathered friend soared into the sky to join the search, his wide wing span giving a hint to his power.

Who would be foolish enough to attack any Ramsay on Ramsay land? Had this man not heard the tales of Logan and Gwyneth Ramsay and their offspring? He cursed when his feet caught on a pile of rocks, but he didn't slow down. Unfortunately, that small mistake cost him. The bastard leaped on a horse and took off at a frantic pace, one that guaranteed Will would never catch him on foot. God's teeth, he needed to make himself a new pair of boots or travel to Edinburgh to get a new pair. He snorted to himself, simply because he only had one real choice.

He could never take the risk of getting caught in the royal burgh, so he'd have to skin his own animals to make the sides of the boots and depend on his two loyal friends to get the soles from the Ramsay expert. It didn't matter what it cost as long as his identity remained a secret.

He leaped across the next burn, grateful he'd managed to keep his feet dry, and kept moving, trying to gauge how far he'd have to go to be safe. He couldn't risk being seen by any of the Ramsays. They were bound to send patrols out after the shooter, and they could just as easily catch him as the guilty party. His horse was well hidden, but he hurried, knowing how important it was to stay ahead.

His life depended on it.

He sighed in relief when he caught sight of his beautiful horse. After patting the animal's flank, he quickly mounted and flicked the reins. His safety was assured.

Almost an hour later, he came upon one of his favorite caves just off Ramsay land, so he took shelter inside, bending over to catch his breath as soon as he was able.

He'd come much too close to being discovered by Gavin's sister. He was quite certain she'd caught sight of him. How he wished he'd been close enough to see Maggie's blue eyes. What he wouldn't give to be able to see them up close… Maggie Ramsay was one beautiful woman, though she did her best to hide it. Her hair was always plaited in a most unique way with small braids pinned to the top of her head and a long braid in back. She always wore the same thing—baggy tunics and leggings, anything at all to hide the fact that she was a woman. If she wore a brat in the coldest months, it was always a bulky one to hide her sweet curves. If he had to bet, she borrowed her sire's clothing.

He forced himself to stop thinking about Maggie Ramsay and worry about survival. He'd have to stay far away from Ramsay land for a while.

There was no way he'd risk getting caught.

———————

MAGGIE PLAYED WITH ONE OF the braids pinned to the side of her head, a nervous gesture Molly was forever trying to get her to break.

If she didn't play with a braid, she feared she'd throw a dagger, her favorite thing to do. Though it would be permissible to do such a thing out of doors, she was currently sitting in the Ramsay solar off the great hall, waiting for her mother and father to join her, thoughts of her sister's premonition haunting her. What trouble could she have foreseen?

As soon as she could, Maggie would press her about the vision. Molly was in Aunt Brenna's healing chamber with Tormod at the moment. The only thing she wanted to do was sit at her sister's bedside with him, but her father had demanded that she and the lads meet him and her mother in the solar.

While she waited, she forced herself to think of anything but Molly…and her thoughts traveled back to the man in black. One glance had seared his image in her brain. Men did not usually affect her so strongly, especially ones who were reputed to be dark and dangerous.

Was he really the Wild Falconer who had inspired so many tales over the last couple of years?

According to Molly and Tormod, who knew more about the goings on in the Highlands than anyone else in the clan, he'd earned a reputation as a sort of vigilante. He would appear out of nowhere to help others who'd been down on their luck or those who had been attacked without provocation. The stories agreed that he was tall and muscular, swathed in black, and oft accompanied by a large peregrine falcon that rode his shoulder. The beast would swoop down out of the sky to strike terror into the hearts of whatever reivers or vicious animals had landed in the Falconer's sights. The stories indicated he never stayed put for long before disappearing into the woods without a trace. No one knew his true identity—only that he was an expert at hiding. If this man *was* the Falconer, she had an inkling that Gavin and Gregor knew quite a bit about him.

The lads opened the door without knocking and proceeded to close it behind them. Now was her chance to see what they knew about the man in black. Oh, they would try to lie, but she'd get the truth from them. "Tell me about the man I saw."

"Nay. He's asked us to keep his identity a secret." Gavin had a rare serious look that told her he wouldn't be easy to break. She glared at him with a growl before turning to Gregor.

"Nay, I'll not be telling either." Gregor had finally stopped repeating everything Gavin said, but the younger lad still had the annoying tendency of verbalizing his support for everything his cousin said and did.

She continued to glare, though she decided not to retaliate by throwing out the fact that she and Molly were adopted, which meant they were not true siblings, even though she'd known Gavin since he was born. She loved both of the lads dearly, as much as she did her other siblings and cousins, so she wouldn't deliberately hurt any of them.

"I want more information," she ground out. "You know how I make a habit of saving information that could benefit me sometime, like the time you…"

"Do not tell Mama or Papa," Gavin whispered. "Promise me."

"You're a fool if you think they'll not find out what happened out there. Aunt Brenna will know how far Molly fell. And why wouldn't we tell them? There were two men out there, and though they didn't appear to be together, one could possibly lead us to the other. Don't you want the archer to be caught? He could be a danger to the clan."

"Not that."

"Aye, not that," Gregor echoed, falling into his old ways.

Gavin moved over to the door, leaning on it as if that could stop their sire, Logan Ramsay, spy for the Scottish Crown, from shoving the door open and bursting through it with all the grace of a bull after a female in heat, his usual manner.

"Promise me you'll not tell him about the man you saw." Gavin leaned his ear to the door before jumping back abruptly. She didn't need to ask why. Their sire was coming, and if Gavin had stayed in that position, he might have been knocked out cold by the flying door. "Promise?"

Maggie sighed. "Promise for now. Only if *you* promise to tell me more later."

Gavin nodded in agreement, though they both knew he had little choice.

The door flew open with a bang, and their parents burst inside. Maggie's adoptive father, Logan, took a seat behind the laird's desk, while Gwyneth, her adoptive mother, leaned against the wall behind him, crossing her arms in front of her. Logan immediately tipped his chair back, casting his gaze over the three of them, his usual intimidation tactic.

"Gwynie," he said, using the pet name only he was allowed to use. "I doubt that wall needs help standing straight up. 'Tis made of stone this thick," he said, sticking out his arms. "I think 'twill hold without your thin frame propping it up. Have a seat with the rest of us." Though he addressed his wife, the woman he adored no less now than he had on their wedding day, he did not shift his gaze from them for a single moment.

"I'll stand where I like, Logan. You know how I feel about men barking orders at me." Though she spoke her strong mind, her eyes glittered with humor at the comment her husband had made. Maggie glanced at her hands in her lap to hide the smirk she couldn't hold back. After all these years, she still enjoyed listening to her parents' playful banter.

Oh, how she loved her mama and papa… She would always remember the day they'd rescued her and Molly in Edinburgh as the best day of her life. They'd helped Molly first—then returned for Maggie simply because her sister had quietly asked it of them.

Lord, thank you again for sending them to us.

At this point, she could probably stop saying thank you every single day of her life without the fear of being sent back rearing its ugly head. After all, she was seven and twenty and had no intentions of ever going back to England. Never, ever, ever.

Her sire swiveled around to look at her mother, waggled his brow, and said, "But *you* can bark orders at *me* any day, lass. This you already know, do you not?" His grin widened provocatively.

Her mother snorted. "Lass is it today, Logan? Hmmph. Mayhap I will be barking orders at you later."

He winked at her before he spun back around to face the other three in the solar, his smile leaving his face in an instant.

"Tell us what happened," Logan announced, pulling his attention back from his wife to his children and nephew.

Gavin nodded to Maggie, indicating he wished for her to start. "Gregor and I weren't there in the beginning."

Maggie would tell them everything she knew, with two exceptions: the presence of the man in black and Molly's premonition. If her parents knew her sister had foreseen danger for her, they might try to restrict her to the keep. She did her best to hold her tears in check. She would not cry until after this was finished. "Molly and Tormod offered to teach me some of the skills they've learned in their job working for the Crown. We were working on tracking skills when an arrow came out of nowhere. Papa, we'd just searched the entire area. Gavin and Gregor had been quite a ways yonder, which is why it took them a few minutes to help us, but the archer must have been close. I don't know how we could have missed anyone! She was coming across the top of the ravine when she lost her footing. I think she heard the arrow sluice through the forest and it threw her off-balance. 'Twas verra quiet. I turned my head in time to see her fall down the embankment. She hit the side a couple of times before she landed. Tormod ran off to catch the archer. Did he find aught?"

"Nay. Grass had been trampled in spots, but that could have been done by any of you," her sire said. "We've no solid information." And he sounded extremely unhappy about it.

"Who could it be?" She glanced from her sire to her mother, so upset she could barely focus.

"We don't know, but we have already sent a slew of guards out searching the area."

Maggie sniffled and whispered, "Mama, how is she?"

Her mother paced a bit before leaning against the wall again. "She's hurt, Maggie. Possibly a broken arm, and Aunt Brenna thinks she's broken a couple of ribs. She's still struggling to breathe because of the ribs. But she won't know for sure until a day or two."

None of that surprised Maggie, not after seeing Molly in the ravine, but she wanted a more solid answer. She wanted someone to tell her that her sister would be fine. "What does that mean? She'll be all right?"

Logan stared at her. "I don't know much about healing, but I can tell you that if she broke even one rib, she won't be going anywhere for a while. She won't be leaving the keep for a fortnight, at least, mayhap two. And that depends on how badly the ribs are broken and how many."

Maggie glanced from her sire back to her mother, devastated by the news. Imagining her sister unable to leave the keep was like thinking of a bird with clipped wings. "Mama?"

"Aye, that's exactly what Aunt Brenna said. She's down for a while. Brenna's going to give her some herbs to make her sleep in case she needs to straighten the bone in her arm."

Her father turned to her brother. "Gavin, what did you two see?"

"Papa, we didn't see anyone out there who could have shot her."

"And what were you two doing out in the woods?" He narrowed his gaze at Gavin as he folded his hands across his lap, one of his thinking positions. Gavin was eight and ten, about six moons older than his cousin, Gregor.

Gavin replied a little too quickly. "Shooting. Right, Gregor?" He turned to his cousin, who immediately agreed with him.

"Shooting, aye. Just practicing. We didn't see anyone who could have done this, did we?"

Logan tilted his head just slightly to glance at Gwyneth. Her parents had caught on to Gavin and Gregor. She didn't need to stay for the ensuing inquisition.

"Mama, may I go see Molly? Please?"

Her mother nodded, giving her permission to run.

Run, she did, as fast as she could.

CHAPTER TWO

———◆———

THAT NIGHT, MAGGIE SAT BY her sister's side, holding her hand and praying she would awaken soon.
She'd sent Tormod off to catch a couple hours of sleep,
promising to keep watch by Molly's sickbed.

She brushed the straggling hairs back from her sister's
lovely face. Lord, but she'd turned out to be a beauty. Their
birth family had chosen to send them into service when
they were wee lasses, saying they had no choice because
there were too many mouths to feed. Any of their burly
brothers ate twice as much as Molly and Maggie com-
bined, but that fact had seemed irrelevant to their parents.
They'd chosen Molly because her sire had thought her
homely. He'd believed they would never find a man who
would want to marry her.

How wrong he'd been.

Shortly after marrying Tormod, Molly had returned to
England with him to find their family of birth. Maggie
had refused to join them, but she did wish she'd been there
to see the look of surprise on their sire's face when he first
set eyes on Molly. Tormod had later told Maggie that the
man had refused to believe Molly was his daughter. His
daughter, he still claimed, had been a very homely girl.

The very idea of the visit made Maggie shudder. She
hated England.

Her parents had never told her why she had been chosen to go with Molly all those years ago. Her mother had
muttered something about not wanting Molly to be alone.

But she knew better.

Tears tracked down her cheeks as she reflected on the

true reason she'd been given away, something she had never told anyone.

Molly jerked her hand away and squirmed in the bed. "Leave me be. My lord, you have no right to touch me. Leave me be!"

"'Tis me, Maggie. Don't worry. I'll protect you, I promise."

Molly opened her eyes and gazed blankly at her sister, then immediately closed them again. Aunt Brenna had given her a strong draught to put her to sleep in order to tend her arm. She was just a wisp of a thing, able to run as fast as the wind through the forests, and she'd managed to take down one of the most notorious villains in all of England and Scotland with her bow and arrow.

Yet here she was powerless and unable to move out of bed.

Aye, the arrow had missed her sister, but she'd find out who'd done this and make them pay. No one would be allowed to clip her sister's wings.

Molly tried to push herself up, doing her best to get away from Maggie now. "Nay, do not touch her." The next moment, Molly's face swung from side to side as if she were searching for something.

Or someone. "Maggie, you must run. He's after you now. He's a verra bad man."

Though she called her name, Molly's gaze never met Maggie's. "I'll protect you, Maggie. Run, please run. Get away from him!"

The very real fear in her voice caused Maggie's tears to flow faster. "Molly, I'm right here. I'm fine. I'll protect you from him." She had no idea who Molly thought was there, but she had her suspicions. "I'm your sister. I'll not hurt you. Please. I only want you to be well."

Then Molly said the one name they both hated. "Randall Baines, I know 'tis you. Get away from my sister!" Maggie understood at once. Her sister was having visions of Randall Baines, the man who'd essentially owned them after taking them into service. He'd dared to touch Molly inappropriately in Edinburgh and his vicious mother had beaten them. "My lord? Go away, please," she insisted.

Was Molly remembering something, or was she experiencing a premonition? How she wished to ask Molly what she had seen, but she could not tolerate seeing the pain in her eyes. "I'm here. He's not. You're safe, Molly. I'm safe."

Aunt Brenna hurried through the door. "Maggie, mayhap you should go. Whatever she's dreaming, I think 'tis related to you. I'll give her more herbs to help her sleep better. Come back in an hour. I'll stay with her until she gets calm. I don't want her moving those ribs at all."

Maggie bolted out of her chair, staring at her sister as she continued to fight her invisible attacker.

"Maggie, she doesn't mean it," her aunt pressed. "She has no idea where she is."

Maggie dropped her sister's hand and fled. What the hell was she to do now? Her very presence frightened her dearest sister, whom she'd vowed to protect many, many moons ago.

As she tore down the stone staircase out into the cold night air, a sudden realization came to her. There was only one way to fix this. She couldn't just sit by and watch her sister be tortured by visions of the corrupt soul who'd made their childhood a misery. Whether it was a memory or a premonition, she had to find Randall Baines to settle her sister's mind.

The man had been heir to Wingate near the border. If she could find him, she could prove to Molly that he would never hurt either of them again. Many, many years had passed since they'd last heard word of him. He could be dead. Perhaps he was poor and living alone in a small hut, or maybe the authorities in England had discovered the truth about him and he was rotting in gaol.

Any of those scenarios would ease Molly's mind and, if

truth be told, her own. Unfortunately, she could think of no other way to help her sister but the one she dreaded most.

She was going to England.

——◆——

WILL SAT IN THE TOP of a ravine, watching the primary route travelers usually took to leave Ramsay land. He'd almost left his cave earlier, but he'd had a strange urge to stay at the last minute. He'd learned a long time ago to follow those urges, believing them to be a guiding hand from his mother. She couldn't speak to him any longer, but she could still nudge him one way or another.

It was the middle of the night, and sure enough, his instincts proved correct. The distant sound of hoofbeats could be heard. He held his breath to hone his sense, hoping it would help him determine where the sound had originated and where the traveler was headed.

The echo grew across the ravine, so he knew a horse was headed this way. It sounded like there was only one.

He watched and waited, wondering who would be leaving Ramsay land in the middle of the night. Perhaps he was about to catch the villain who had dared to shoot at Molly, causing her fall. Instead, to his surprise, the figure atop the horse was none other than Maggie Ramsay.

She was alone.

He raced to his horse, mounting in seconds, and followed her at enough of a distance that he wouldn't be noticed. Following people without being detected was his area of expertise. He'd followed some for days without being discovered.

Gavin and Gregor had told him that Maggie was even tougher than her elder sister, if that were possible, and she was deadly with a dagger, her aim perfect with every throw.

Even so, where in hell was she headed in the middle of the night alone? Such a thing wasn't safe, regardless of the lass's obvious strengths.

He followed her, surprised at her stamina, through the forests and the valleys. Never once did she look behind her. Maggie was definitely on a mission, and he doubted anything would deter her. She rode her horse for most of the night without stopping. Her horse had to be lathered, so he was pleased to see her finally slow to search for a place to rest. Once she finally settled in a cave, he found another spot not far away in a clearing. He wasn't worried about not catching her in the morning. She'd have to pass him, and since he was such a light sleeper, he was quite certain he'd wake up as soon as she passed. Then he would need only to jump on his horse and follow.

Except that wasn't quite how it went.

He'd just finished chewing on the last oatcake in his satchel, still in the clearing, when he found himself flipped onto his back with a dagger pressed his throat. Maggie's face hovered a mere hand's length above his own.

"Who the hell are you?"

The tip of her blade pricked his neck. When had his senses ever been so slack? He'd heard nary a twig snap or the swish of a leaf.

She had her weight thrust against his chest while she straddled him.

God's teeth, but the blade was not the only thing playing havoc on his senses. If she straddled him any lower, he'd be totally undone.

He forced himself to focus on the dagger. "How can I answer with that dagger piercing my skin?" He gagged, not intentionally, but due to the pressure she kept on his windpipe.

She let up a touch. "Speak. Who are you and why are you following me?"

"Will MacLerie. Friend to your brother Gavin and his cousin."

"What clan?"

"Nae clan. I live on my own."

"Where?"

"Wherever I choose. I travel the land as needed."

"Are you the Wild Falconer?"

He couldn't help but react to that, but hopefully he'd recovered soon enough to keep her guessing. "What if I am?"

"Why Gavin?"

"He taught me how to better use a bow. He's one of the best besides your sister." He detected the slightest change in her grip, just enough to give him the chance he wanted.

With one smooth movement, he flipped her onto her back and lay across her, pinning her in place, her dagger tossed off to the side.

"Get off me," she whispered, the fury in her voice palpable. She wriggled beneath him, only to stop abruptly as soon as she noticed his hardness against her belly. "You're a pig," she spat out.

"I didn't start this, lass. You threw yourself at me, if I recall correctly. I don't know what you expected to happen when you plastered your fabulous curves against me, but you must know you're a beautiful woman."

And her fists came out. She fought like a caged animal. He let her up but did not let her go, instead twirling her around and holding her back against him. "Relax. I would never attack you—not in any way. I apologize for my verra male reaction to you. I'll let you go when you promise not to cut my throat with your dagger. I'm sure you have another one on you."

"I promise not to cut your throat with my dagger."

The fury still raged through her body, so he held on to her, feeling the sudden need for one more promise.

"Promise not to cut my bollocks off either."

CHAPTER THREE

———◆———

MAGGIE GRINNED, SURPRISED THAT HE'D caught on to her intention so quickly. Though she still struggled against him a chuckle erupted from deep in her belly.

"You are the daughter of Gwyneth Ramsay. Did she not just kill the man who kidnapped her daughter by pinning his bollocks to a tree?"

"Aye, 'struth."

He spun her back around to face him, holding her pressed against his body. "Can we not talk? Will you agree to that before you try to slice me again? I could help you. I want to help you." He gazed into her eyes, a silence growing between them.

"You wish to help me because you're the Falconer? They say you're a vigilante, out to help those who've been wronged. Is that so, or do you run outside the law because you're evil?" Facing him, a strange feeling blossomed deep in her belly, something that heated her insides, making her very aware of his presence, of his body—of *him*.

"I'm not a vigilante. If I see someone I can assist, then I do. 'Tis simple."

"Yet you hide. You never speak with anyone. Why?"

"I don't need to speak to anyone."

Standing this close to him unsettled her. He smelled like the outdoors, like pine and horse and sunshine. Or was it his heat that reminded her of the sun? Either way, the color of his eyes called to her—bright blue and green with a multitude of dancing colors within them. He had a dangerous look to him, yet she wished to trust him. His gaze held hers—unflinching, unwavering. Was he telling the truth?

"And the falcon?"

"I have trained a couple of falcons to travel with me occasionally. They don't do my bidding. But one will stand on my shoulder or land on my arm. If that makes me evil, then I guess I am."

She took in everything about him. He had a strong, almost forceful, presence, but she did not feel threatened in any way. His hair was long and untamed, his beard a short stubble across a strong jawline. In fact, everything about him was dark except for his eyes. They were like the eyes of wolves in the black of night, seeing all and knowing all.

For some reason she could not understand, she trusted him.

"You haven't answered my question. Do you promise not to slice me in two?" He stared at her, his grip pinning her to him. Her nipples peaked as he studied her, awaiting her answer.

The silence discomfited her, so she cleared her throat and said, "Agreed." His eyes had transfixed her, and a small part of her was disappointed when he finally let go of her. How had she not noticed how handsome he was before?

Then she quickly reminded herself that she wasn't interested in handsome men.

"So Will MacLerie, why are you following me?" She retrieved her dagger and replaced it in the sheath at her waist.

She bent over to check the ones attached to each of her boots—and caught him bringing his gaze slowly up her legs when he thought she wasn't looking.

She was. Any other man would get a dagger in his thigh for such audacity. Why not him? And yet she found herself eager to hear what this man had to say. She stood up and turned around to face him. "So, tell me more."

"I've already given you all the information I can. You know my name. I live in the woods. I prefer to be called Will rather than the Wild Falconer. I introduced myself to Gavin and Gregor one day, and they've been training me for a while now. I have no family, so I go from place to place."

"Why me?"

He settled back onto the log he'd been perched on when she first attacked him. Damn, but he was bigger than she'd thought.

"I followed you because I was worried about you. Think of me as your protector." He yanked on a piece of bark jutting out from the log, breaking it into pieces before he threw the handful of waste off into the distance. "I have naught else to do, so why not follow you? You are Gavin's sister. Does he know you're out here alone?"

"Nay, and promise me you'll not go back to tell him, or I will cut you when you sleep." She moved over to stand in front of him, her hands on her hips. His gaze traveled up from her feet to her leggings to the hands on her hips before finally jumping to her eyes. He'd better not cause trouble for her.

"Do your parents know you're here alone? If not, I think we may be making a bargain, lass."

She cursed inwardly at his comment. "What do you want from me? It better be appropriate. Remember whose daughter I am," she drawled.

"Where are you headed?"

"None of your concern."

"Then I guess I'll be heading back to Ramsay land. I'm sure your sire would be more than pleased to find out where you've gone." He stood, his chin jutting out with confidence as he pulled his sword from his horse and sheathed it behind him. He winked at her again. "This is for my own protection."

"I'll ask you again. What do you want?" She couldn't let

him go to Ramsay land yet, not when she'd gotten this far. If she just had a little more time, she'd be able to guarantee her sire wouldn't catch up to her before she completed her plan.

"To travel along as your protector."

"Why? Why don't you just go home?"

He spread his arms wide. "This is my home."

"You've no parents? No family at all?"

"Only my grandsire is left, and his hut is only big enough for one. I lost my mother three years ago. I have naught else to do but protect my friend's sister."

Maggie glared at him. Damn, but he had her there. She'd left in the middle of the night. Her sire would never have willingly allowed her to travel alone, especially not to the destination she had in mind, Gavin and Gregor still feared Logan too much to test his boundaries. She'd left a note to her parents in the kitchens, knowing no one would find it until morning. By the time they did, she'd be well ahead of them.

Her fears about her sister had carried her this far, but she had to admit a few new fears had popped up in the night. Aye, she was strong, and she had no doubt in her ability to defend herself, but everyone knew it was a bad idea to travel alone, for a lass *or* a lad.

"How do I know I can trust you?"

"You saw me the day Molly went down. Gavin and Gregor were working with me, helping me improve my shot. We sparred with swords a bit, as well."

"Why haven't we met before? I practice with them often."

"I prefer to stay hidden, but I broke my silence to introduce myself to your brother and cousin. Doing so was risk enough. They promised to help me and keep my identity a secret. In return for that favor, I offer my services of protection to you. Mayhap I'm not as strong as your sire, but I'm getting there, and you know two fighters are better than one."

"Why must they keep your identity a secret?"

"That's *my* secret." He crossed his arms, so she guessed he'd given her all the information he was willing to divulge.

"Are you any good with a sword?"

"Better than passable. I have naught else to do but train with my bow and my sword."

She tipped her head to the side, staring into the trees. Could she trust him? She trusted her brother and cousin completely, and they seemed to have faith in this man. "All right. I could use some help. I may have left prematurely, but I won't go back until I find what I seek." She held her hand out. "I'll keep your secret if you keep mine."

He shook her hand and said, "Agreed. One more thing. As I said, I'd like you to pledge to keep your dagger away from my bollocks."

She broke into giggles, but then the thought of her sister surfaced in her head—Molly lying hurt in that bed, frightened out of her mind—and she stopped in an instant. "You must promise not to touch me inappropriately. You understand my meaning."

"Lass, I don't hurt women, nor would I ever rape one. But I'm happy to make that promise to you. Where are we going?"

"To England. Just over the border to Wingate. I want to find Randall Baines. He's the son of an earl. I haven't seen him in nearly two decades, but I know where to find his castle. I won't have a plan until I know more. We'll start there. We leave at first light."

Will nodded, heading toward the bushes, but then stopped to call out to her over his shoulder. "I'll be right back. And, Maggie, please remember one thing."

"What?" she asked, puzzled. Hadn't she given him what he wanted?

"I'm a man of my word, so when the time comes that you want me to kiss you, and it will, you'll have to make the first move." He winked at her again and strutted off into the bushes.

Arrogant bastard. What had she gotten herself into?

CHAPTER FOUR

TWO DAYS LATER, THEY'D ALMOST made it out of the Borderlands, and Will was at his wit's end. He'd tried his best to convince Maggie that he was trustworthy, but he was clearly wasting his time.

He'd been quite excited at the prospect of traveling with a beautiful, spirited woman. In truth, he was tired of spending so much time alone. The more time he spent with her, the more time he wanted to spend with her—surely there were no other lasses as bold and brave and beautiful as she—but if he'd thought anything would come of it, he'd been dead wrong. Maggie Ramsay was a focused warrior who was not to be distracted from her mission. She also didn't talk much—at least not to him.

They sat on a log at dusk, chewing on rabbit bones. Fortunately, she was as good with her bow as she was with a dagger, so they'd eaten well. "MacLerie, you don't look like you're enjoying our time together." She grinned as she wiped the juice from her chin.

"As long as we're almost there. This has been an uneventful journey."

"Shite, don't say that. You'll curse us." She glanced over her shoulder as if some creature were about to jump out of the tree at her. "We'll be there on the morrow, though mayhap not until midday. Not exactly sure how far 'tis from here."

He glanced over into the bushes as if in search of something.

"Allow me to guess your troubles. Did you wish I would

wash my hair and leave it hanging down my back all pretty? Or maybe that I had a gown packed inside my satchel to wear for you?"

He couldn't help but chuckle at the image in his head, Maggie dressed in a lovely gown with her hair still tied up in those practical braids, a dash of dirt on her pert nose.

"And why do you laugh?"

He sat in the grass, tossed his bones off and leaned back on his elbows. "Because that's not who you are, Maggie Ramsay. I hadn't given a thought to how you'd look with your hair down."

"I'm not like most lasses."

"I can see that. Many lads work their arses off for many moons without gaining the skills that seem to come so naturally to you. I'm sure you've practiced long and hard to get them. You're also loyal, hard-working, and your mind works quicker than most men I know."

She stared at him for a long moment, as if seeing him in a different light. "My thanks. I didn't think you'd noticed."

"How could I not? We've been traveling together for a couple of days now. But there is one other quality you possess that the people around you cannot help but notice, no matter how hard you try to hide it."

"What?" she asked, her forehead wrinkled in conster-nation.

"Your beauty. I think you wished you weren't. You're lean like a lad, but you cannot hide your feminine grace. You run like the most graceful creature I've ever seen, and yet I think that side of yourself embarrasses you. But you cannot hide it. My question is why would you try?"

She stood up as though insulted. "Enough talk. I haven't tried to discuss any of your qualities, so leave mine be. I'm not interested in your opinion. Whenever you've had enough of our travels or my company, feel free to head home."

"As you wish." If only she felt differently…he'd listen

to her insult him if only to hear her talk. He watched her move over to her horse to grab a cloth before sitting on the log again. Maggie Ramsay was the most intriguing— and most beautiful—woman he'd ever met. Not that he'd ever been in love. He was seven and twenty, and the situation he'd lived in for the past two years had prevented him from ever staying in the same place long enough to have a relationship with a woman. Sure, he'd kissed many women, even had the pleasure of feeling the softness of a woman's skin in his hands, but he'd rarely completed the act.

Many times he'd regretted his lot in life. Part of him would like nothing more than to have the chance to love Maggie Ramsay in every way possible—to stay in one spot, maybe even marry her and live on Ramsay land.

But that wasn't the path chosen for him. No one had thought to ask him what he wanted.

MAGGIE TOSSED THE BONES OFF into the bushes and headed out of the clearing. "Going to wash up in the burn."

How she hoped he wouldn't follow... She feared she wouldn't be able to hold her tears inside. When she swiped at her cheeks, she wiped away the single droplet that had already escaped.

Being attractive to men caused nothing but trouble. She'd seen what it did to other lasses, being saddled with curves, soft lips, and all the things that made some men lie. So she did whatever she could to make herself unattractive to men in the hopes of keeping them at bay. While a part of her wished for the kind of relationship Molly and Tormod and her parents shared, she doubted she'd ever be able to have what they did. How many men could handle a lass who could throw a dagger better than anyone in her clan? How many men besides her sire and Tormod wanted a strong woman, one who could think and hunt and run as well as a man? She knew what most men thought of women.

Besides, her job was to take care of her sister. She owed Molly more than she could ever repay her. Her sister had always protected her. Whenever Maggie had dropped a pitcher of goat's milk or didn't sew fast enough, Baines's mother or housekeeper would take a switch to her. Only Molly would never allow her to take her due punishment, instead begging for double just so her wee sister wouldn't have to be punished. Of course, they'd always made Maggie watch.

How guilt had eaten at Maggie when she was small. Each day she'd fretted that she would make a mistake and her sister would suffer because of it.

A squeal broke into her thoughts and she spun around, grabbing for her dagger, but she was too late.

A wild boar was headed straight for her, its sharp jaws wide open and ready for her. Many large warriors were killed by boars. She wouldn't stand a chance...

Will yelled, "Maggie!" just before he launched himself at her, catching her by the waist and knocking her to the ground. He landed on top of her, but the boar sailed on past them.

They both lifted their heads to see where the beast had gone, only to catch sight of five other animals coming from the same direction, all headed straight at them. Will covered her with his body as the beasts approached them, wrestling and nudging one another. She felt nothing, only fear.

The animals reared and squealed as if annoyed with them for trespassing on their land. They trounced and kicked, turning away and rushing back toward them, as if purposefully playing with their senses. Maggie's entire body was rigid, scared to death that a set of teeth would grab hold of either one of them and yank them apart. Will tightened his grip on her and dragged her under a nearby rock, shielding them as best he could from the beasts and their gnashing teeth. And yet they still kept ramming them—an endless tirade of unhappy, hungry boars—until Will unsheathed her dagger at her waist and plunged it into the belly of the closest creature, sending him squealing in the opposite direction. Suddenly, a flurry of flapping wings and squawks surrounded the other boars, which confused the beasts and sent them running off in the same direction as the injured one.

As quickly as the birds arrived, they departed.

Once the boars retreated, Maggie did her best to calm her breathing. Will still held a firm grip on her and he leaned in and whispered, "Are you hurt?" his breath warm against her ear.

"Nay, I think not." She pushed far enough away from him to scan the area for any animal that might be waiting to attack. When she felt safe enough, she rolled over to face him. "Will, you must be hurt. They were brutal."

He shook his head. "Nay, I'll probably have a bruise or two on the morrow, but I'll be fine. Are you sure you're not hurt?"

The paleness of his features caught her. He was still panting, but this wasn't the reaction of someone who'd just escaped a dangerous situation. This was the type of breathing a person would do if they were hurt. "Will? You don't look so good." Up close, he was more pleasing to the eye than ever, but something was badly wrong. She shifted away from him and sat up.

He remained on his side, but his hand came up to guard his flank. That was when she noticed the blood. "Oh my, Will." She tugged his hand away. "One of those beasts bit you." She could see the teeth marks through his tunic. Getting up on her knees, she leaned over him to search for more bites on his back, his legs, anywhere.

This man, whom she'd spent the last two days pushing away, had probably saved her from death, and he'd been mauled in the process. She scrambled to her feet, grabbed one of the clean linen strips she kept in her pocket, and hurried over to the stream to dip it into the cool water. "Will, are you all right? Say something, please."

When she returned to his side, he stared at her, his eyes a little glazed over, but he was alert. "I'll be all right, Maggie. Don't worry."

"I'll clean the wound. I have some poultice in my satchel that my aunt always uses for wounds to stave off the fever. Here, can you hold your arm up for me?"

He did as she asked, his eyes following her as she took her dagger out to cut his tunic away, removing the shredded part of his garment off from the rest. She used the linen to wipe away the blood, cleaning what she could. "Maggie," he said, staring at her with those bright, beautiful eyes, "there's a clean tunic in my satchel. Grab that and I'll take this one off so you can use it to wipe the blood away."

"Aye, but first we need to move you."

Working together, she got him to his feet and guided him to a nearby tree so he could lean against it. Once he was settled, she ran back to the horses, careful to make sure there were no boars in the area. When she returned, he'd already removed his tunic and was holding the material against his wound. "My mother always said to keep pressure on a wound to stop the flow."

"My aunt says the same." She nodded in approval. After returning to the burn to cleanse the linen strip, she knelt in front of him and…

He reached for her hand.

"I'll be fine, Maggie. No need to panic."

But she *was* panicking. This was just like when Molly used to take her beatings for her. She'd always nursed her sister's wounds afterward, though it had done little to remove the sting of knowing someone had been hurt for her. *Instead* of her. "You protected me. I owe you a debt of gratitude. Many, many thanks to you. The boar you stabbed came straight at me. He would have bitten me, mayhap killed me…" she continued to ramble until his finger came up to her lips.

"Hush. You've thanked me, but I didn't do aught you wouldn't have done for me. Would you clean it one more time? I did roll on the ground after the beast wounded me, and there was much dust in the air. My mother always said to get the dirt out, otherwise it becomes a permanent part of you."

"Was your mother a healer, then?"

"Aye. That part was always bothersome to me. I feared I'd have a patch of grass growing out of my back if I wasn't careful."

She laughed, cleaning the wound as best she could. "I promise to get the grass out. It doesn't look as bad as I thought now that the bleeding has slowed. What else can I do?" She pressed his hand to the wound, the piece of tunic directly atop it so it would soak up any more blood.

"Talk to me?" he asked. "I feel a little dizzy."

"Just a moment. I'll be right back."

She returned with the poultice and the skin of ale they'd been saving, choosing to drink fresh water instead. "Here, drink this while I put the poultice on. I have another strip of linen I can use to bandage it. I think 'tis long enough to go around you."

She set about her task, but caught herself as soon as she reached behind his back. She found her face close enough to kiss the smattering of dark chest hairs in front of her face. Forcing herself to continue as if it hadn't affected her, she brought the linen around, now completely aware of the muscles in his body, the hardness of the planes of his abdomen, the sheer beauty of him.

Hell, but she'd never been so aware of a man before. Her entire body heated at the closeness of him, but he appeared oblivious, or mayhap he simply chose to ignore the obvious by closing his eyes.

All of a sudden, everything changed about Will MacLerie.

CHAPTER FIVE

———————

THAT NIGHT, MAGGIE AND WILL found shelter in a different cave he recalled from a previous journey, hoping to distance themselves from the boars. While he claimed the dizziness had passed, the pain of his bite had to be increasing from the bouncing over the rough terrain. A cave would protect them and give him the rest he needed. When she moved her horse toward the cave, she was pleased to see it was small enough that they could tie a rope across it to deter unwanted visitors, especially wild boars.

As soon as they dismounted, Maggie caught sight of a flock of geese headed their way, so she pulled her bow out and brought one down.

"Nicely done, Maggie," Will said as he dismounted and hurried over to grab their dinner. "I've had more than enough rabbit."

She bounded after him. "I think I missed the larger bird."

He held it up for her to see. "Bigger than any I've caught recently. 'Twill feed both of us with ease."

They worked in silence. While Maggie settled the horses and gave them each some oats, Will prepared the goose and built a fire just at the edge of the cave, well away from the most traveled route.

They ate as if they hadn't eaten in days. Maggie produced a small hunk of cheese to add to their meal. "We worked hard today. How is your wound?"

She could see he did his best to hide the pain, but he replied, "I think 'tis much improved."

Rather than object that he was lying or, at the very least, exaggerating, she simply gave him a doubting look. Then she recalled something. "The birds. After you stabbed the boar, did I not hear a flock of birds nearby?"

He shook his head. "Not a flock, just the two falcons. The peregrine is the fastest bird I've ever seen, and it can deliver quite a blow to any animal. The smaller one isn't as powerful, but the two tend to travel together."

There was no denying his past fascinated her. While he clearly didn't want to tell her about what had set him running, mayhap he'd at least tell her about his time as a vigilante. "So are all of the tales of the Wild Falconer true?"

"And what tales have you heard? I rarely talk to anyone other than my grandsire, your brother, and your cousin, so I don't hear much. Tell me more." He got up and took care of the fire before propping himself against the mouth of the cave.

"Did you kill a wolf with your bare hands?"

He hesitated for a moment and then asked, "How do you hear such tales?"

"Did your falcons peck the eyes out of a man trying to steal your horse?"

This time he laughed heartily. "Nay. Where do these stories come from?"

"My sister and her husband work for the Crown. They travel often. There must be some truth to the tales. Did you save a lad who was falling down a ravine?"

"Aye. 'Tis true. I was at the base of the ravine when I heard his scream. I was in the right spot at the right time, and I managed to catch him before his head hit a boulder. His sire was at the top of the ravine watching."

"But you didn't stay to speak with him?"

He chewed on a bundle of mint leaves, offering her a few. "Nay. I set the lad down, asked the man who he was, and when he said he was the lad's sire, I left."

"Why?" She hated to push him because he looked

exhausted, but she'd never felt this curious about another person. What motivated him? What did he wish to do with his life?

"Because I was no longer needed. The lad was awake and moving, and I knew his sire would take care of him. 'Twas all I needed to know." He bent his knee and rested his arm on it, shielding his wound.

"Why do you hide?" She didn't expect him to answer, but she couldn't help but ask. This was the most important question of all to her. Who was Will MacLerie?

"I'm not ready to share that with you, lass." His eyes fluttered shut, but he opened them again.

"Are you an outlaw? Do you run from the sheriffs?"

He stood abruptly and grabbed his satchel, pulling out a fur and two plaids. "I can no longer keep my eyes open. My apologies, but I must sleep." He handed her the fur and one of the plaids. "Here, these are for you."

She took the two items and thanked him. He held his hand out for her and helped her to her feet. What he did next surprised her more than anything. He leaned over and kissed her cheek. "You need not worry about me doing aught inappropriate. I'm too exhausted."

As soon as he settled on a spot inside the cave and rested his head on the rolled-up plaid, his eyes closed and his breathing took on the rhythmic sound of someone in a deep sleep. She found a spot not far from him and did the same, covering herself with the fur.

She closed her eyes with a smile on her face. The plaid's aroma was all Will and she found it oddly pleasing, almost as much as the warmth of his lips on her cheek.

———◆———

THEY HADN'T GONE FAR THE following morn when they came upon a family of travelers. Since they hadn't seen any other riders this far into the Borderlands, they stopped them for information.

Maggie motioned to Will so he would speak first. "Can you tell me how far we are from Wingate Castle?"

"About two hours ahead. The vendor fair is on all day. The earl is not currently in residence, but many of his men are around. Mind yourselves. There's a toll and they mete out punishment for any small transgression. Blood thirsty the bastards are."

Will thanked him and they moved ahead. "Maggie, we need to discuss a plan, do you not agree? Are you just going to the gates to demand entrance or what?"

"We're in England, not the Highlands. There will be many people milling about, especially with the fair going on. They'll not even notice us. We can hide amongst the visitors."

"You must have more of a plan than that."

"I need to find out where Randall Baines is at present. I'd like to speak to the man. That's all you need to know. If he's in attendance, I will request an audience with him. He's the earl's son, so I expect him to be present. He's likely acting in his sire's stead, and from what I know of him, he's the blood thirsty one they speak about so candidly."

"Are you going to tell me what your interest is in him?"

"Sure. He's a no-good piece of shite, something I would prefer to scrape off my shoe."

Will nodded. "Saints above, that was amazingly helpful. I know just what we're doing now."

She couldn't help but laugh, something she seemed to do a lot of around Will. "I'll let you know more when we're closer. How is your side? I should probably change that bandage later." How was it that she already felt so comfortable around this man? She couldn't deny she trusted him, which usually did not come easily for her. She glanced at him from the side, hoping he wouldn't notice. There was something about him...something that made her want to be closer to him.

How odd. How she wished Molly were here to give her

advice. She shook her head to send that stray thought away. There was a purpose to this journey, and she would not be waylaid by a man.

He waved his hand at her. "I already changed it. 'Tis much better. I can hardly feel it at all."

They came over a small hill, and to Maggie's surprise, they could see most of Wingate from where they stood. The bleak stone building, smaller than either the Ramsay or Grant castles, loomed front and center, as if expecting anyone coming from their direction to bow to its majestic presence.

The curtain wall touted many guards, a testament to the supposed value of the nobility residing inside its walls. She knew the castle to hold a bailey inside, with all the buildings necessary to support castle life, but the gates were well guarded. No one unsuitable would be allowed near the Baines family.

A cobblestone courtyard had been added in front of the castle, an oddity to any Scot. The vendor booths had been set up within it, flying colorful flags advertising their goods, mostly food and some weaponry, to all who were in attendance. The set up would have been considered unusual in Scotland. Clans celebrated on the inside courtyard with the noble family except in times of large festivals.

Maturation illuminated this world to Maggie. She had thought the fortress impressive and intimidating when she was a young girl, but it fostered different feelings and thoughts now. As they guided their horses along the outskirts of the fair, her gaze took in things she'd not noticed as a child of six or seven summers.

At her cousin's annual dog festival, she'd challenge anyone to find a face without a smile. Not here. There was no laughter amongst the throng, instead people moved along quickly, their banter only meant to hurry the person in front of them. At Wingate, Randall Baines's father presided over the peasants like a tyrant, and it showed. She saw worry and fear etched on faces as young as twelve summers. The mostly gaunt crowd hustled about while men with beady eyes watched their every move, waiting to swing a blow to any unsuspecting person for any supposed affront, supposed crime.

There were no children.

When that caught her attention, she scanned the area again for anyone under the age of ten, but there were none.

Only one thing caught her eye—a starving puppy searching for scraps. It endured kicks from any boot it dared to come near, and its high-pitched yelps moved no one to drop a morsel of food.

They found a place to leave their horses and made their way through the throngs of people. To get into the vendor area, they were forced to pay a toll.

"Who is it we're paying?" Will asked. "I've not seen a toll here before." How small she felt next to him. His dress drew a few glances, but she doubted the Falconer's reputation had traveled this far south. Still, dressed in black, his hair long and untethered, he commanded attention.

She noticed something else about Will. Anyone without a weapon made sure to stay several paces away from him.

So why did he hide?

The guard, clearly annoyed, retorted, "Pay up or the earl will have you take a few straps in the middle of the courtyard like the others."

Will paid the fee, but Maggie was distracted, drawn to the cries of a thin, brown-haired lass whom two burly men were dragging toward the center of the crowded cobblestone courtyard. A cackling woman, dressed like a housekeeper, followed them. The wee lass was forced to bend over a large rock in the middle and the large woman grabbed a switch from the assortment that had been laid out. "This one is a tough one. It'll take many lashes to make her cry."

The lass kicked and screamed against the two men who

easily held her down and tied her hands to the pole opposite the rock.

The housekeeper clearly liked being the center of attention, though many of the people turned away, as if they'd
seen enough torture inflicted on wee ones. But other people drew closer, attracted by the housekeeper's bellows.

What made people enjoy the punishment of others?

The woman continued to unfurl her drama for all to see.
"My lord Baines insists on order within his walls. If you
steal, you'll pay the price," she announced loudly enough
for all to hear. She snapped the switch against the pole for
emphasis. "This girl broke a bowl this morn, one of our
best. She'll get her just due for being slack at her job." She
swirled her skirts as she made her way over to the lass.

The lass, quite feisty, said, "You are the lazy one, Mistress.
This is the only job you enjoy."

"Silence!" She brought the switch down across the
back of the lass, who never made a sound. The girl wore a
threadbare garment, so there was no doubt the bitch had
broken her skin…and yet there were no tears on her face.
Her expression was filled with a fury Maggie had never
seen in a child so young.

The sound of the switch hitting the girl's body trans-
ported her back—back to a time when it was *she* who
wore the threadbare gown. Twenty years ago, that lass
could have been Molly, though the housekeeper had never
disciplined them with a crowd around. Things had gotten
worse at Wingate Castle.

Molly had been so stoic, taking beating after beating
with barely a whimper. She swiped at a tear, hoping she
could regain control of herself without relenting to the
deluge that threatened to cover her cheeks. Usually the
torment would end with Molly soundlessly crying.

Randall rarely took part in the beatings, but he made
it his business to check on all those disciplined within
Wingate Castle. Most of the young women feared some-

thing else entirely—the earl's son would offer to dress their wounds and then use it as an opportunity to touch them.

It would seem the bastard hadn't changed a bit. He still encouraged his help to whip young ones. And that housemaid or whoever she was deserved her just due no less than Baines did.

I'll do what I can to pay you back, Mol.

Maggie could tolerate it no longer. She said to Will, "I'm going over there to put an end to this cruelty. Be ready. I'm not leaving without the girl. Watch my back and then run for the horses." She didn't wait for his agreement, just set out to do what she knew she had to do.

She climbed to a spot behind a tree—a place where she'd be hidden from the crowd down below but would have the perfect vantage point from which to take aim. She waited until she saw Will following her and then fired without hesitation.

Her first arrow hit the woman's right shoulder, the arm that held the switch, forcing her to drop it with a howl. The second arrow hit one guard's side, and then she removed one of the daggers from her boots and threw it, hitting the other guard in the leg. None of them were mortal wounds, but the villains would not be able to make chase.

Maggie didn't wait to take advantage of the chaos that ensued. Charging forward toward the courtyard, she shoved bystanders and gawkers out of her way so she could grab the girl. She sliced her bindings loose and carried her out of the crowd before anyone could think to stop her. The girl stared at her with wide eyes, but she ran along with her willingly enough. Anything to escape the scene of her torment.

Maggie sprinted, weaving in and out of the crowd. Will had opened up a path for them, his size and pace intimidating the onlookers. The wee one's hand clutched hers in a death grip as they raced toward the horses. Though Maggie didn't let it slow her down, she broke out in a smile at what she saw lay ahead of her.

The Wild Falconer had a soft side. He paused for just a moment, pulled his arm back to deliver a blow to a man who'd kicked the puppy she'd noticed before, then bent over to scoop up the starving creature and stuff it inside his tunic.

A few moments later, shouts of, "Get them!" reached her ears. But Maggie didn't stop, she pulled the girl along behind her as she ran to her horse. Will stood ready to assist, and she shouted, "Put her behind me so I won't hurt her back." As soon as he'd helped the two of them mount, he leaped atop his own horse in seconds.

"Don't worry, they'll not catch us," Maggie whispered to the girl over her shoulder.

The lass looked terrified. "Who are you? They'll kill you and beat me harder." The tears she'd held back during her punishment finally dripped down her cheeks. "I don't think I can take any more beatings."

"Trust me. I'll see that you never have another. My sister received many a lashing within the confines of that castle, and they won't abuse you any longer." Maggie flicked the reins, shouting, "Hang on," as they took off behind Will back toward the Borderlands.

They had traveled for about an hour when the sounds of pursuit caught her attention. She glanced over her shoulder, whistling to Will to be certain he noticed.

The three men behind them immediately fired a volley of arrows, each of which missed by a large margin. Their ineptitude was amusing, but should any of their arrows fly true, the lass would be the first one hit.

She could hear them shouting, so she did her best to catch their conversation.

"We've got them. The earl will pay us big if we bring them in. A little more and we'll be on them."

"Dead or alive? I can easily shoot the two lassies, but what about the big one?"

"The Falconer? We'll never catch him, but we can make good with the lassies. Let him go."

She had to save the lass. They'd surely hit her first, and she couldn't risk it.

Finding a hiding place behind a copse of trees, she saw another hidden spot nearby and pointed, shouting at Will to take cover. He followed her lead and, without hesitating, pulled out his bow and launched an arrow at their pursuers. She was pleased to see he'd taken out the leader. Maggie readied her bow and took the second man out, then downed the third with a dagger to his chest.

All three fell off their horses and no one else followed, so they took off again. Though it didn't appear any of them were dead, they were likely too injured to follow. With any luck, they could reach Scottish soil before nightfall.

The day was almost gone when Will led them off the main path toward a clearing near a small stream to water their horses. Finally halting the animals, they listened to see if they were being followed. All that echoed in the forest was the crisp sound of squirrels scampering through the treetops.

Was it her imagination, or did the air just smell sweeter on Scottish soil?

Maggie and Will exchanged a nod—no one was about—and Maggie dismounted and helped the lass down. "Do you think they'll follow us?" she asked Will. She only hoped they hadn't killed any of them. If they were the earl's men, she could face consequences.

"Nay. They were reivers. Must have heard about our visit to the fair and decided to exploit the situation. I'm sure they're familiar enough with the earl to know they'd be paid well for bringing us in, but I doubt they'd be foolish enough to follow us onto Scottish soil. The savage Scottish reputation carries far onto the land of the English."

She was surprised to see her wee companion still had tears on her face. As soon as the lass's feet hit the ground, she launched herself at Maggie's middle, wrapping her arms around her in a fierce hug. A moment later, she pulled back to stare at Will. "Are you the Wild Falconer?"

Will gave Maggie a stunned look, then turned back to answer the lass, but words seemed to have escaped him.

Maggie said, "That one reiver *did* call you the Falconer... I suppose your reputation has spread farther than we thought." She shrugged her shoulders and grinned just as a furry bundle popped up out of Will's tunic. The pup shook his head, his big ears flapping with the force of his swing.

The lass squealed. "You brought my favorite puppy! I thought he died already."

"You recognize him?"

"Yes. He was in a litter of six pups. He was the biggest. I think the others died because they were sent out to fend for themselves when they were too little."

Will set the puppy down and he ran straight for the lass, his tail wagging. After delivering a series of licks, he ambled to the burn for water.

The lass followed the puppy with her gaze before turning back to face them. A fierce look burned in her eyes, and Maggie could tell she would prove to be a strong-minded person. "Many thanks. I appreciate what you've done, but will you help me? The earl stole my sister." Tears slid down her cheeks as she stared up at Maggie, new hope in her eyes. Her gown was not just threadbare but dirty, and she took off her cap and threw it into the trees. Her brown eyes spoke of intelligence and cunning. "I hate the earl and all who work for him. They're horribly cruel."

The spark of hope in the lass's eyes caused a slew of emotions to bubble up in Maggie. Hatred and fear and, worst of all, uncontrollable rage. She willed them away, not wanting to ever go to that evil place again, but every glance at the lass set the feelings churning deep inside her belly. She stepped back and closed her eyes, squeezing as much as she could to stop her own tears from appearing on her cheeks. This lass didn't need any more dark emotions…she needed someone to encourage that last bit of hope.

"What's your name?" Will came up from behind Maggie, settling an arm around her shoulders in a strangely comforting fashion. To her shock, she felt no desire at all to pull away.

"My name is Simone." The lass swiped at her tears before folding her hands back in front of her. The way she did it spoke of habit.

Prim and proper, just the way Baines's housekeeper had always insisted.

Fold your hands in front so I know you're not stealing.

Will continued, "Well, Simone. You'll need to tell us more before we can assist you. There are only two of us, so I know not how we can chase across all of England in search of one lass, especially when we have you with us. We only have two horses."

A tear slid down the girl's cheek but she didn't look away. Nor did she back down. "If you cannot help me, then take me back. I'll not desert my sister. She's all I have." Her hands were still folded in front of her, gripped so tightly together that they were whiter than the clouds in the sky above them. "Even though she's no longer there, I could learn more about her there than I'm likely to here."

She's all I have.

Saints above, nothing could have pulled at her more than that expression. Maggie had felt that same way for years. Now she had family and friends, cousins galore, but there had been a time when Maggie and Molly had stood alone against the cruel world. Och, she knew what it was to love a sister.

Maggie whispered, "Tell me more about your sister."

"My sister was whisked away in the middle of the night, and I know not where they've taken her. I must save Beatris. She's only five summers, just a wee thing. They took her away and refused to tell me more, and I...I...I must follow her." Maggie stepped closer and reached for her hands. "Our parents gave us to the earl to work his kitchens. He...he said he liked to take siblings because they could be used to control each other, but he never said he'd send us away. I hate my parents for selling us to him."

"How old are you?"

"Ten summers, but I'm much stronger than Beatris. She's younger and sickly because they never feed her right. I think 'tis why he sold her. She's not as hardy as I am."

"Listen to me. I've been there before. My sister and I used to work for the earl. She took my beatings for me because I wasn't strong enough. Those people are cruel, the earl, his son Randall, his housekeeper..."

Simone gave her a puzzled look. "Randall *is* the earl. His sire died a year ago, but he's worse than the old earl. He has me beaten more than the old earl did. When the old earl died, many of his workers left. Randall brought in new people—crueler ones."

"Beatris was four when your mother sold you to the earl?" Maggie had to ask the question, though she dreaded the answer.

Simone nodded. "I do not think she cares if she lives or dies. She used to be so full of life, now she only smiles for me," she whispered, "and I've lost her."

Maggie closed her eyes, dropping Simone's hands so she could pace, something she often did when she had new information to absorb, especially if it was something she hated. She'd never been as quick-witted as her sister, instead needing time to sift through information before making an important decision. What was their next move?

She wanted more than anything to save wee Beatris. She'd have to put her own need for vengeance aside to help these lassies. There had to be a way to find Beatris and save her...

But how?

The bastard was now the Earl of Wingate with all the power it carried with him. She'd not be able to kill a member of the English nobility without serious repercussions. She had made certain to only injure his men. Mayhap she had connections to the Crown in Scotland, but she could be hung if accused of murder in England.

Part of her had hoped this mission would be simple. That she would come to England and discover Randall Baines had been stripped of his power. She'd hoped to find him destitute. Such a thing would have empowered her to return home, tell Molly how badly the man had fallen, and hopefully cheer her. Even better, she could have discovered he'd fallen from his horse and died. Or that someone had justly killed him years ago.

This new information would not help.

Discovering Baines's success—and the fact that he was still using it to hurt people—changed everything.

Will interrupted her thoughts, firing questions at Simone. "Where could they have taken her? How long ago? Know you of his regular travels?"

"He took her away a sennight ago," the lass said, rubbing fresh tears off her cheeks, "and he hasn't been back since. I've been trying to find out where he went by sneaking through the tunnels at night to listen in on the servants' conversations, but the only thing I know for certes is that he brought her to the royal Scottish burgh. I think Edinburgh, but I'm not certain. I don't understand. Why would he sell my sister? Even though she was sickly, she was a good worker."

Maggie glanced at Will, wondering what his thoughts were about this new information.

It didn't matter.

Maggie had a new goal in life. She'd save Simone and her sister, just as Molly had saved her.

The earl would be next.

CHAPTER SIX

RANDALL BAINES, THE THIRD EARL of Wingate, stood inside the upstairs chamber of his Edinburgh estate, his hands on his hips, pleased to see the three girls cowering in the corner as loyal subjects should do.

The castle's housekeeper, Eda, the lazy cow, stood staring at the three of them. "What shall I do with them? These three are young'uns…"

"Find them some broth and a loaf of bread. We'll be traveling soon. Clean them up, too."

He could hear the bitch sigh over his instructions as he left the chamber. Ignoring her muttering, he entered the hall and made his way toward the hearth to pour himself an ale. But the door flew open before he could reach his destination. "Men here to see you, my lord," one of his servants blathered. He didn't remember the man's name. "Said it's important."

What now?

He trudged out of the small castle after the servant. It wasn't an overly large estate, but it was plenty big enough to hold the servants and whoever traveled with him. He wasn't fond of the Scots, in truth, but they were such savages that it was easier to hide his trail here than it was near London. Once he made it to the firth, he would have nothing to worry him. The population of the coastal village was so unpredictable that they paid outsiders no attention at all. He would be free to do whatever he wished with his merchandise. He needn't even worry about being seen boarding them.

The visitor, Captain Granville, was the head of his guard, which meant it had to be something serious. The man had served both him and his father, and because of his dedication, Randall had left him home to handle Wingate in his absence. The man waited with Gerold deVere, Wingate's marshal, who had made the trip with Randall. The servant who'd led him out to see the visitor scurried away like a frightened mouse.

"What's the problem, Granville?" Randall asked.

Granville motioned for them both to follow him into the stables, and once they were inside, he closed the doors to prying ears. "I do not wish to be overheard."

That got his attention. "What is so important you needed to follow me here?" he asked.

"Problem at the castle. Your main housekeeper was injured, one of our men is sick with the fever, and the other cannot go back to his work yet.

"What the hell?" he blustered out. "Had you no protection for my castle? It's your job to protect everyone." His eyes blazed, even though he did his best to narrow them.

"It happened on market day. Someone hit the housekeeper in the shoulder with an arrow while she was attempting to discipline one of the housemaids. The young girl has also disappeared. Two of my men assisted the housekeeper—one took an arrow in his side, and the second took a dagger in his leg. His wound has festered and he's been ill with the fever. I've lost two fighting men and the mistress is still bellowing about killing the girl. She's more ornery than a bristling hedgehog that hasn't eaten in days."

"Arrows? Are you sure?" He couldn't believe anyone in his village would have the bollocks to shoot his men. Though he didn't give a shite about the woman, shrew harpy that she was, shooting two good warriors was punishable by death in his kingdom.

"I came because of what the villagers are saying. They

said it was a woman and a large man, all dressed in black."

"And you came here to tell me that?" Baines wished to slap his men silly sometimes. Why did they bother with the smallest of details, making them into something he should worry about? He was the earl, after all, and no one would ever attempt to stand against him. He had the King of England on his side, didn't he?

His marshal stared at him in disbelief, so he was clearly missing something.

"What?"

"That sounds like the Wild Falconer. Have you forgotten?" deVere asked.

Granville nodded in agreement. "That was my thought. I believed it to be my job to make you aware of the problem."

"The Wild Falconer? Who..." He stopped to think, pushing his memory until it finally came to him. "The one who has hundreds of birds at his mercy? Killed a wolf with his bare hands?"

"Yes. That's who the villagers believe attacked us. Some say the woman fired the arrows, but his image has struck the fear of the devil into them. They can barely function now, looking over their shoulders at every bird call."

Baines had to think about this one. He'd send someone out after him. True, the Wild Falconer was reputed to be one of the most savage Highlanders of all, even more so than Alexander Grant, but he had his doubts. No one could best the might of an English earl. "I appreciate you traveling this far to advise me of this possibility. I'll give this careful consideration before I make any plans. Do you have any other information for me?" He downed a swig of his ale.

"I brought one of the arrows for you. Do you recognize it?" He handed it over to the earl.

Randall Baines grabbed the arrow in a rage, but as he examined the shaft, a sudden jolt of recognition brightened his day. He turned it over in his hand, and a broad smile crossed his face, though he hated to smile in front of any of his men.

"You know it?" deVere asked.

"I do for certes. Only one clan in Scotland uses these types of feathers for their fletching. That bitch carefully forms each one herself, and they even use a special blue dye to color them. Without question, this proves to me that we were attacked by a specific clan. Well done, Granville. This is all the proof I need to go to our king." He spat off to the side. "Those savages will pay for this. You said two are dead?"

"No one has died. But two men are currently too disabled to work. Not exactly dead, but of no use to us at the moment."

"Never mind. I don't wish to hear any more. As far as I'm concerned, one died from this arrow...and I cannot wait to dole out some vengeance in the Highlands."

"But what about the Wild Falconer?"

Baines snorted. "I'm not worried about some fool with a bunch of birds. What I have in my hand is much, much better. I've been waiting to pay these bastards back for what they did to me."

DeVere smirked knowingly. "Ah, tell me it's so."

Baines flipped the arrow up into the air, catching it with a smug smile of gleeful satisfaction. "This is a Ramsay arrow, and I vow to make them pay for this atrocity."

———

WILL LED THEM TO A well-hidden cave several hours later. "We can sleep here. It should be another day before we reach Ramsay land." To his relief, Maggie had agreed to return to Clan Ramsay before continuing on to find and stop Baines. Though he was not at all eager to leave Maggie, he did not think they could manage this alone. Surely her parents would send someone else with her. He needed to check on his grandsire, so he would leave her as soon as they reached Ramsay land. If anyone could help Simone find her sister, it was the Ramsays.

His part in this adventure was at an end.

"Do you think we'll make it before the sun drops?" she asked. "I must speak with my sire at once."

"Aye. As long as the good weather remains, we should arrive a couple of hours before sunset." He set down the puppy, who quickly scampered off into the bushes.

"Will someone there listen to you?" Simone asked.

"Aye. We also need to get you new clothing. What you have on should be burned."

Simone stuttered out an inaudible response, but then stared at the ground, her face red.

"What is it? 'Tis not your fault the earl does not see you properly dressed."

Simone cleared her throat before staring at the ground. "Would it be possible for me to wear clothing as you do? What you wear looks much warmer than what I have on, even though 'tis lad's clothing."

Will choked, and Maggie swung her head around to stare at him, a question on her face.

"What?" he asked with a shrug. "I hardly think you look like a lad in your clothing." He turned away, knowing Maggie would be discomfited if she could guess at his thoughts...and his admiration. She filled those leggings unlike any lad he'd ever seen, her hips curving sweetly and her long legs giving him thoughts that refused to be silenced.

True, at first he'd viewed this trip as nothing but entertainment. How often was he able to talk to a lass as beautiful as Maggie Ramsay, much less travel with her? But the more he learned about her, the deeper his feelings grew. She would do anything to help an innocent in need.

Maggie fought harder than anyone he'd ever met, making him take a long hard look at his own values. True, he'd helped others when he could, but had he ever risked so much?

Not like Maggie Ramsay.

He heard her answer Simone. "Aye. 'Tis what my mother prefers. She is the finest archer in all of England and Scotland, or at least she was when she was young. She says you cannot fire arrows well if your hands get caught in your skirts. We have plenty of leggings and tunics for young lasses in our clan. I have a sister and a cousin near your size."

The puppy flew inside the cave and landed on Simone's lap, who promptly giggled. "What shall we name him?" She glanced at Will to see what his response would be. "We never gave him a name at Wingate because we were afraid he wouldn't make it."

He clapped his hands and the animal raced over to him, tail wagging. Will picked him up and cuddled him into the crook of his arm. "Do you have a suggestion?"

Simone shook her head. "I think you should name him. You saved him."

"He's your companion, Will," Maggie added. "You've been chosen by him."

"So I have." Will picked him up, stared at his black fur, and said, "Angus. My companion."

Simone said, "He's all dressed in black, just like you." Simone lifted her gaze and smiled, an expression that transformed her face, making her instantly look younger. Then her face turned glum. "Do you truly think someone there will help me?"

"Aye, my clan will help you. As I've said, my sister and I were in the same place and my mother got us away from the earl's people. She and my father adopted us." She chucked Simone under the chin. "I promise you. They will help us, and so will many others."

Will found a couple of small logs and brought them into the cave, motioning for Maggie and Simone to sit down.

"Are you warm enough?" He brought his satchel inside and tossed a plaid to Simone. "This should help. Get situated so we can plan for the morrow."

Maggie sat down, though she waited for Will to settle before she began. He'd felt her thaw toward him these past couple of days, something he savored. "You may not know this, but there are several people in my clan who know Edinburgh verra well."

"What would you suggest we do?" Will asked.

"I'm hoping my sire knows the location of the earl's castle. Once I check on my sister's wellbeing, I hope to convince my parents to travel with us. I can bring several Ramsay guards. We will not give up until we find your sister, Simone, I promise you. Will and I will convince my parents…"

"Nay, not Will and I…" Will forced himself to whisper. Och, he liked the sound of it, but there could never be a Will and Maggie, not even in this.

Maggie scowled. "What? You will return with us, aye?"

"Nay, I cannot, Maggie."

Maggie's gaze narrowed, but she said nothing. He couldn't tell her the true reason he wasn't going with her. He truly couldn't.

"Why not?" Her face changed in an instant, shutting down, and he felt the wall between them ice back up. "Never mind. If you've done all you care to do to assist us, I'll handle the rest myself." She grabbed her own satchel and pulled out two oatcakes, handing one to Simone and chewing on the second one herself. "I understand if you must go elsewhere. Simone, I will get us help from my clan."

Simone gave Will a pitiful look. "You're leaving us?"

"I must," he said to Simone, pretending to fuss with a thread on his breeches. "Maggie will see that you find your sister."

"Why don't you come with us?" she asked. "You helped

us get away from the bad men."

"I'm not known in this area and I would prefer to keep it that way. Besides, I have someone I need to see. Maggie and I just met before we came to the Borderlands. I was in the area when her sister was injured…'tis why I came along on the journey. She and her clan will take care of you and your sister. I can promise you that."

Silence settled between them. He waited, a small part of him wishing Maggie would beg him to travel with her to the burghs. He could possibly arrange to meet her somewhere, but he would not risk meeting her parents.

Though he couldn't explain to her, he would be risking both of their lives if he broke his vow to stay hidden.

THE FOLLOWING DAY, MAGGIE COULD feel her insides churning the closer they came to Ramsay land. She prayed that Molly was better. She didn't expect her sister to be well enough to travel with them, but she hoped she was at least moving around the keep. Whatever the case, she had no doubt that Molly would support her in her new goal to pursue the end of the current Earl of Wingate. Randall Baines did not deserve his noble title. And if they could find Beatris, they could adopt the two lasses into Clan Ramsay.

When they were about an hour from Ramsay Castle, Will motioned for them to stop. He dismounted and then pointed to a patch of trees. "I'll not be going with you the rest of the way. Godspeed to you."

Maggie didn't know how to respond. Had he not traveled with her, her journey might have had a tragic end. She could have been caught at Wingate or skewered by one of their pursuers. He'd had her back all along.

And the incident with the boar? She'd never forgot how bravely he'd saved her…nor would she forget how it had felt to be so close to him. While he had given her a small kiss on her cheek, it didn't seem like enough. His words suddenly came back to her. *"When the time comes that you want me to kiss you, and it will, you'll have to make the first move."* Would she have another opportunity?

On impulse, she jumped down from her horse and ran over to him, placing her lips against his in what she hoped would be a welcome kiss, a kiss meant to let him know how much she'd appreciated his presence on her journey. She pulled back and cast a quick glance up at him to see how he'd reacted to her kiss, but instead he reached for the back of her neck and tugged her back for more, teasing her with his tongue until she opened for him, allowing him inside. A multitude of sensations flooded her as he plundered her mouth, a small growl greeting her. His lips were warm, and he tasted like the forest and the mint leaves he'd recently chewed on. The heat of their embrace shot through her senses, scorching her insides until she thought she'd explode.

This…this was what it was like to kiss a lad you really wanted?

As quickly as he'd started the kiss, he ended it, giving her a quick smirk. "That's how 'tis done, lass."

He spun on his heel and left. The puppy's face popped up over his shoulder as he departed, and she couldn't stop herself from waving to the wee creature.

Maggie hurried back to her horse, mounting from a nearby rock. As soon as she was settled on the saddle in front of Simone, her fingers involuntarily reached up to her lips as if to implant his taste in her mind forever. A quick glance back at the lass told her that her companion was as confused as Maggie by what had just happened. Her eyes stared at the ground to the side of their horse.

Maggie patted her hands and said, "You're about to meet my clan. Trust me that you'll love everything about Clan Ramsay."

They were close enough to Ramsay land that she felt

comfortable flicking the reins of her horse and sending them off into a nice canter across one of her favorite meadows. The sun was out, reminding her that spring was in the air, and the birds were busy chattering while the red squirrels scampered from tree to tree. She loved the Highlands, though some said the Ramsays weren't actually in the Highlands since they were so close to the border. It seemed like a bunch of nonsense to her. The mountains could be seen in the distance.

As soon as they drew near the gates, Gavin and Gregor came out to greet them, a few guards trailing behind them.

"Where have you been, Maggie? Papa has been looking for you. I'll give you fair warning. You'd best don a coat of chain mail before you go through the gates." Gavin had that smirk on his face he often wore when he thought he knew more that she did, so she chose to ignore him. This was not the time for jesting. He picked up on her demeanor quickly, changing the flavor of his questions. "You are well?" Gavin asked before he peeked behind her. "And who is that?"

"This is Simone." The lass looked down at the ground, staring at it as if she hoped she could disappear into it. "I'll explain later. How is Molly?"

"Mama and Papa are furious you left alone." Gavin quirked his brow at her and Gregor grinned.

"We told them you'd be fine. No one can throw a knife like you, Maggie," the younger lad added.

"I'll deal with them. I had my reasons." She nodded to the guards, who had now turned to escort the two of them to the gates.

"Papa just returned," Gavin said. "He went after you but never caught up to you. How could that be?" The lads wore matching grins, reminding her of how they'd always gotten each other in trouble when they were lads of four and five summers.

"I'll talk to him, Gavin. He'll understand." She ignored

him and continued on through the gates and to the stables, where she dismounted and then helped Simone down. "The only explanation I can give you is that I was so upset that I was not thinking clearly. You're right—'twas dangerous to go alone. I did, however, meet one of your friends."

Gregor glanced at Gavin, wide-eyed. He hadn't yet learned to hide his feelings. He was honest to a fault.

Her brother, on the other hand… "Which friend would that be, Maggie?" Gavin pressed. "We have many. One of our numerous female friends? You know I have many lasses begging for my attention."

She snorted at her brother as they all made their way to the keep, Simone next to her and holding her hand, moving closer to Maggie whenever the lads drew near. "Must you always amuse me so? You have no lasses chasing you about."

"Are you sure about that? Have you taken a good look at me lately? I've grown into a fine man of eight and ten. The lasses, that is, the beautiful ones, do adore me. Poor Gregor," he announced, glancing over his shoulder at his cousin. "He just waits in my shadow, hoping someday he'll be able to find a lass for himself." He flashed her a beautiful white smile.

"Och, you're not homely, but 'tis all I'll give you, *lad*." She drew out the word to remind him of his age.

"I am the only son of the beast of the Highlands, and word is I look just like my sire."

"Huh. I'd never noticed," she teased. "What about Uncle Quade? Gregor has his eyes. I've heard the lasses talk of *him*."

Gregor's chest puffed out, but he said nothing. Gavin said, "He knows who draws the eyes of the lasses."

She chortled. "In your mind only." She peered at Gregor, now smiling from ear to ear, and shook her head. "How can you bear to listen to him for hours on end, dear cousin?"

As soon as they reached the courtyard, her father's growl

could be heard across the way. "Where the hell did you go, Maggie? And without saying a word to anyone? That note was hardly an explanation." He was stampeding toward them, but he came to a sudden halt, his gaze fixed on Simone.

Simone's tiny hand held Maggie's hand in a death grip. "Papa, this is Simone. She was about to be beaten in the middle of Randall Baines's courtyard, but I decided to put an end to it."

Logan Ramsay flinched at the mention of Baines's name. Wherever he'd thought she'd gone, he clearly hadn't guessed correctly. Simone jerked her head to the side and buried her face in Maggie's tunic. "He's so angry. Please do not let him beat me." She turned her head to peek at Logan again before hiding her face in Maggie's clothing.

She glared at her father. "Papa, please?" He'd always had a raging temper, but never would he dream of raising a fist to a lass in anger. Once he put his anger aside, she knew the man she loved and trusted would emerge.

Logan froze, his gaze taking in Simone's tiny shaking form, and his entire countenance softened. He nodded to Maggie, the fury in his face gone in an instant.

"Forgive me. Simone," he whispered, "I promise you'll never be beaten here. This is my sire's land, and my brother's and my nephew's. None of us would ever allow anyone to take a strap to a child here."

Simone pulled her face away from Maggie's side. "Greetings, my lord," she said in a small voice.

Logan recovered quickly, though Maggie knew she'd be asked to answer for her actions later, as soon as Simone was safe and out of hearing. Everything would be fine once she explained the situation.

Her father almost put his hand on the lass's back, but Maggie shook her head vehemently, hoping he'd get the message not to touch her there. She'd been struck once, and Maggie could see how she guarded her back. She hadn't asked to look at it because no blood had seeped through and she'd feared embarrassing the lass. But she'd be certain to have Aunt Brenna tend to her soon.

"You two must be hungry," her sire said softly. "Come inside for something to eat. You can sit near the hearth and warm up. We'll have plenty of time to talk later."

"How is Molly, Papa?" she asked as they made their way toward the hall.

"She's improving. We have her seated in front of the fire. Her ribs still pain her something fierce, but we have managed to finally get her out of her chamber. 'Twill be a while before she's able to ride a horse again. She's missed you." He gave her a look of censure over Simone's shoulder, but she chose to ignore it.

"Is Mama inside?"

"Aye, she's with Molly. Jennet is playing healer and Brigid prefers to sit by your mama's side."

A jolt of emotion shot through Maggie, surprising her. She directed her attention to Simone. "Jennet is my cousin and Brigid is my youngest sister. Jennet is your age and Brigid is but a year younger. You'll get to know them both." How she'd missed everyone. They continued into the great hall in silence, and as soon as they entered the door, Gwyneth bolted out of her chair and greeted Maggie with a fierce hug. "Where have you been? We've all been worried sick about you." Her gaze dropped to Simone. "Oh. Who is this sweet child?"

"I'm sorry to have put you through the worry. I'll explain everything in a bit." She led Simone over to an empty chair near the hearth, close to Molly. Her mother followed her, as did her wee sister and Jennet.

As soon as Molly's gaze caught hers, her sister gasped and said, "Maggie. I'm so glad you're here. I was so worried about you." She paused to adjust her position a wee bit, taking the time to rearrange the fur on her lap. "Who is with you?"

The pain in her face when her sister moved still bothered her. "Molly, Mama, this is Simone. I found her in a terrible situation, so I brought her home. She would like to join Clan Ramsay." Simone still clung to her hand, so Maggie patted it. "Brigid, would you find something for Simone to eat? Jennet can assist you."

The two took off toward the kitchens, eager to do their part for the newcomer. Maggie reached for her sister's hand. "How are you?"

Molly's gaze lifted to hers. "Better. 'Tis hard to breathe—" she slowed, taking a few shallow breaths before she continued, "—but I improve every day. Aunt Brenna thinks my arm may be sprained and not broken. Where have you been?"

"I found Simone at the whipping post at Wingate Castle," she said. There was no way to soften the words. "She was about to be disciplined for accidentally breaking a bowl."

The tears slid down Simone's cheeks.

Molly didn't miss her reference. In a small voice, she asked, "Wingate Castle?"

Maggie met her sister's gaze and nodded, then glanced back at her sire. "Simone and her sister, Beatris, were sold to the Baines family. Randall Baines, the current earl, moved the wee one out of the castle to sell her. Unfortunately, Simone doesn't know where she is, though she suspects she could be in Edinburgh. She's verra worried about her because she's only five summers. I told her our clan would gladly help her. Isn't that correct, Mama?" She had no doubt her parents would agree, but her mother might not want to leave the castle with Molly still so ill.

Her mother's eyes misted. Molly gave a slight gasp before she whimpered from the pain of breathing in, or so she guessed. Her sire hadn't moved a muscle.

Maggie knew what that meant. He was doing his best to control the fury overtaking his body.

Simone whispered, "Will you help me find my sister? Please?"

Logan said, "You can count on it, lass. Now tell me everything."

CHAPTER SEVEN

WILL RODE THROUGH THE FOREST as fast as he could, riding through part of the night. He had to make it to his grandsire's, get his advice, and then hurry back to follow Maggie. He knew she'd be heading out within the next two days to pursue the earl and guessed they would go to Edinburgh.

He followed the hidden path to his grandsire's small cottage hidden in the woods, a good two hours from Ramsay land. Once there, he hopped down from his horse, tethered the beast to a tree, and made his way to the front door. As he knocked, he found himself hoping his grandsire was not off visiting somewhere.

His grandsire swung the door open with a start. "William, 'tis good to see you. Come in, lad, come in."

Will gave his grandsire a warm hug, being careful not to knock him over. His grandfather was in his sixties, something rare in their area. He hadn't shaved in a decade or more, so his beard flowed down his chest. On occasion, Will would walk by and clip a section off just because it annoyed him. His grandpapa always bellowed and swatted his hand.

"I need it to keep the bugs away," he would defend himself with a grin. He kept his hair shorter because of the curl—he said he often felt as if he had a thousand pigs' tails pinned on the top of his head. His mind was still as sharp as the needles on the tall pines surrounding his home, though his eyesight and his bones were failing him of late. Will visited him often enough to cut wood for him and make sure he was well, but then he would leave, fear of being caught overtaking his desire for companionship. There was a nearby cave where he slept at times, especially whenever he was worried about the dear man. The older man took his measure and said, "You need clean clothing. I'll find some for you."

"Grandpapa, I've been busy, but I've come for advice and I've not much time. Will you help me?"

His grandfather's mind was as spry as ever, but his joints pained him something fierce. He moved slowly about the cottage, motioning for Will to take the seat closest to the hearth as he puttered about, finding him an ale. After handing him the drink, he settled into the seat opposite him. "I had hoped you'd return soon. You know how I enjoy your visits, lad. Grab a bowl of mutton stew for yourself or you'll waste away to naught." He waved toward the pot hanging over the fire in the hearth. Tipping his head closer toward Will, he muttered, "Though it appears you're bigger and taller every time I see you."

Will suddenly noticed his hunger, so got up and filled a bowl for himself. "Would you like one?" The puppy popped his head out to stare at his grandfather.

The old man smiled. "What have you there, William?"

"Just a wee scavenger I picked up along the way."

"He's not been fed well, has he?" He knew that look on his grandfather's face. He was an animal lover at heart.

"Here." He tugged the dog out of his tunic and set him on his grandsire's lap. "Keep him warm while I eat. Are you sure you don't want something?" Will found a bone and handed it to the puppy to gnaw on.

His grandsire shook his head and waved him off, petting the squirming animal on his lap. "I can eat whenever I like. I keep it warm. 'Tis safer that way, as you know. Now, tell me what brought you back. Are you missing your mother as much as I am?"

"Aye," he said, taking a bite of the stew as he thought of

his dear mother. "How I wish it could have happened any other way, but I have no regrets. Except I wish I hadn't been forced into hiding."

"Is that blood I see on your tunic, William? Remove it and allow me a look."

Will groaned, but he set down the stew and gave in to his grandfather's request because he knew he'd have his way eventually. "I had a small battle with a boar."

"And my guess is he won. Those are teeth marks, I see. How long ago did this happen?"

Will didn't look his grandfather directly in the eye, because he knew what was coming. "Not long."

"Hmmm. You're being intentionally vague, yet someone took good care of the wound. Else it would have festered." He scratched his chin and said, "Must be a lass."

Will rolled his eyes. As much as he loved the man, he hated that he was usually right about everything, managing to draw correct conclusions from very little information. He shrugged his tunic back into place. "Grandsire, I met someone along the way and traveled with her as protection. Gavin's sister."

His grandsire quirked his brow. "A Ramsay lass out alone? I commend you for protecting her. Apparently, you ran into the boar and saved her from its jaws. Boars can leave nasty bites."

"Aye, there was a lass with me. Her name is Maggie, and she treated my wound with a salve from the Ramsay healer. The Ramsay healer is as good as they say she is."

His grandsire's finger came up to point at him. "That pleases me. Mayhap you can speak with Logan or Quade Ramsay and convince them of your innocence. The right person could speak to our king and demand leniency."

"I'll prove my own worth somehow."

"You're just like your mother. Stubborn as a bee with a waggling stinger aiming to do its job. I just hope the Mac-Ewans don't catch up with you."

Will bolted out of his chair. "They won't. Stop saying it, Grandpapa. I've never witnessed aught as cruel as my mother's death. I did what I had to do. You know I'm right."

His grandfather held his hands up, his usual calming gesture. "Relax, lad. No one will know you're here but you and me. You've naught to fear."

"Don't I?" he asked, running a hand through his hair in frustration. He started to pace the small space, avoiding the unfinished stew he'd set on the floor. "Apparently they've forgotten that I was with Mother when *it* happened. They may have forgotten, but I haven't."

"Lower your voice, son." He sighed. "I fear you are right. They'll forget eventually, but 'tis too early."

Silence settled between them. Will returned to his chair.

His mother had been a healer, but not the usual type found in Scotland. She'd possessed the amazing ability to begin the healing process with naught but the heat of her hand. One day she'd found a young lad in the woods with an arrow through his belly. The lad was barely breathing and unconscious, so she'd decided to take a chance…

What followed still filled his nightmares. It always would.

"William, your mother could no more have walked away from that lad than she could have stopped breathing. Her gift was a part of her, and she was proud of it. She couldn't just watch him die, knowing she could save his life."

This was a conversation he and his grandsire had had at least two dozen times, yet he still found himself reacting the same way. Saying the same things.

"Why wasn't I more careful? If I'd seen them, everything would have happened differently."

"Do not put yourself through this again. Fate brought those men out to witness your mother do her beautiful work."

"Beautiful work it was. Why did no one else view it that way?" He and his grandsire stared into the flame under the pot in the hearth. It hurt to think of that day. The worst day of his life. "Have you discovered aught? Is there any chance they'll soften toward me? They were in the wrong. She tried to do them a favor…"

"And she saved the lad's life."

"Aye," he said simply because it was true.

"The boy undoubtedly had no idea what had happened to him," his grandfather said, "so he could not give them any information. I told you what I think the fools did."

"Aye, Grandpapa. You think one of them shot the lad by mistake."

"Aye, and by accusing your mother of witchery, they took the attention away from the guilty party."

Will leaned back in his chair, staring at the beams above him.

"I have a different question for you, lad. I wonder why you healed so quickly from the boar attack."

"Don't make this into something it isn't, Grandpapa. I'm not my mother. I'm not a healer and I don't have any special powers. I only wish to be like everyone else—free to go where I please. There must be something I can do…I'm tired of running, tired of hiding."

"Then stop. If you hide yourself in the cave near my cottage, no one will know. You could live there for years without being discovered."

"But 'tis not the life I would choose. I could be a Ramsay warrior, train with the best, travel the Highlands. I could have worked for the Crown like Maggie's parents. Instead, I must hide from everyone."

"You're right, lad. 'Tis no life for a young one. You're a strong, vibrant boy who has much to offer. If you've met the Ramsay lass, mayhap you can request a meeting with her sire, explain all that happened and see if he could help you."

How he wished he dared to tell someone about his situation. He lived in fear of dying like his poor mother had.

He was haunted by the image of her engulfed in flames. The men had called her a witch when they'd seen the boy heal in front of their eyes. They'd cursed and sworn and beaten her...and then they'd set her on fire.

His own mother had died right in front of him. He'd lived with that image in his mind all day, every day, even when he slept.

Except for recently. Something else had dominated his thoughts of late, and it was a welcome change—a lass with brown braids and sweet lips and an aim better than most lads. "Grandpapa, I've met someone." He stared into the fire again, wondering how much he should admit to the old man.

"So you've already said, the Ramsay lass."

"Aye, but she's different." He didn't know how to put his feelings into words, so he hoped his grandpapa could understand what he was trying to say.

"She means more to you," the old man said, nodding slowly, folding his hands across his growing belly. "I knew that would happen someday, but I'd hoped 'twould not be for another year or so." He leaned back in his chair and sighed deeply. "You must be verra careful. I've told you that many times over. Naught has changed."

Aye, he did know that, but it wasn't going to stop him. He had felt *normal* while traveling with Maggie Ramsay. "I'm drawn to her like a moth to the heat of a flame," he admitted.

"You need to be careful or she'll burn you."

He jerked his head to glare at his grandsire. "Can you not be happy for me? I think the lass returns my feelings."

His grandsire sighed so loudly he started coughing. "You need to find one that's not part of a noble family. Should you find a lass who lives in an isolated hut on her own, I'd be ecstatic. Until then, tread carefully." His bony finger came up to point at him that way he liked to do so often. "The Ramsays are well known, and they're favorites of

King Alexander. Mayhap they could help you, but they could also hurt you."

"I have a question for you."

"Good. I have one for you. What is it about her that caught your eye?" His grandpapa waggled his bushy eyebrows, which seemed to take on a life of their own whenever they moved.

"She's from Clan Ramsay and 'tis all you need to know. Now I'll ask mine. Have you heard of any nobility selling bairns?"

"Selling bairns?" his grandpapa asked in alarm, leaning forward in his chair. "Is this a jest of some kind?"

"Nay. We came in contact with a lass of around ten summers who thinks her sister is being sold. She spoke of an English earl. Know you aught about it?"

"Nay, lad. But I know just who to ask. Change your clothes, eat hardy, and go on your way. I'll be leaving as well. If you visit again in another day or two, I'll have an answer for you."

"You think you can uncover something? Who will you ask?" Will suddenly felt the need to meet his grandfather's neighbors. They kept him informed on nearly all that took place in the Highlands.

A gleam came into the older man's eyes. "Never you mind. I may be getting on in years, but I have my secrets."

"I promise to return, Grandsire. Travel with care."

He'd return to the Ramsays to see what Maggie's plans were, but he would definitely come back here to see his grandfather. He couldn't help but smile.

The wily old goat was up to something.

CHAPTER EIGHT

SIMONE'S EXHAUSTION SHOWED FROM THE way she happily went to bed with Jennet and Brigid in the lassies' chamber. Molly had fallen asleep in front of the hearth, so Tormod carried her upstairs to their chamber. It pleased Maggie to see how gentle and loving he always was with her sister.

As soon as the others had gone to bed, Maggie's parents summoned her to the solar. Her father drummed his fingers on the desk, taking his time to begin his interrogation. Gwyneth sat next to him.

She wasn't going to wait for his usual intimidation games to begin. "Forgive me for acting so rashly. I was undone by Molly's condition. When she thought…" Visions of Molly swinging her one arm at her, thinking she was Randall, brought her back to the powerlessness she'd felt that night.

Her mother whispered, "Your Aunt Brenna told me your sister thought you were Randall Baines."

"Aye, she did, Mama. How was I to react to that?" She bolted out of her chair to pace, but also to swipe at the tears she didn't wish for her father to see.

"In your note," her father said, "you said that Molly had a premonition, too. Would you explain that please? She has no memory of it."

"One thing she said was that I had to run, that someone dark was going to hurt me. I don't know if it was a premonition, or if she was merely remembering what happened to us so many years ago. I knew the king sent that man back to England, but I thought it would ease Molly's mind if I could locate him, prove he was no longer a threat to either of us." How could she convince her sire she'd done what was right? Perhaps she'd been a bit hasty, but all had gone well.

"So you thought you could travel alone at night and kill him? Was that your master plan?" Her sire leaned back in his chair, setting his boots up on the desk. The farther back he leaned, the louder his voice became. "Did you leave with any plan at all or did you just set out with your emotions churning in your gut, the worst time to act?"

"Nay, that wasn't my intention. I was hoping no action would be necessary…that I'd find him destitute and alone. Or dead. But I don't know…mayhap I would have killed him if it came down to it." Her voice came out as a shout, but she didn't care. "I couldn't keep her from falling down the ravine, but I could keep that bastard from bothering her again."

"Maggie, I know you and your sister were treated horribly, but why not let it rest? I cannot believe you traveled to England alone."

All of a sudden, she had a revelation.

Her sire hopped out of his chair to stand in front of her, his hands on his hips. "What is it?"

"I just thought of something. Do you suppose Molly's premonition was about Simone and Beatris instead of me? Could she have foreseen something happening to Beatris? If so, we have to make haste."

"Randall Baines is now an earl who answers to the King of England. If he is doing aught to lassies other than training them to work in his kitchens or as housemaids, he could lose his title. I don't think he's that foolish."

Maggie stared at her father, as if glaring might impart all her memories into his mind so he could see what she had seen every day. "Randall Baines has no conscience. Allow me to remind you what it was like for us to live with him. Every time I made a mistake and was to be punished, Molly would beg for double the strokes to prevent me from ever feeling the lash myself. Every time! Once I dropped something three times in one sennight. Her bottom was almost raw. He deserves a dagger between his eyes." She could no longer prevent the torrent of tears from washing over her face, though she did her best to wipe them away with her sleeve. "We lived in fear every moment of our days. After all these years, his memory is still the first thing to haunt her when she's hurt. Does that not tell you something about him, Papa? He's a monster, a cruel, unfeeling monster."

"Maggie…" her mother said as she walked over to wrap her arms around her. "Your motives are honorable…"

She fell against her mother and sobbed, all the stress of the last several days finally bursting from her.

"And just," her father added. "That bastard doesn't deserve his title. But why didn't you ask for help? You should never have gone alone. Any number of Ramsays would have gone with you."

"I didn't go alone." She picked her head up enough to answer her father.

"Who went with you? One of our guards?" Her sire glanced at her mother.

"Nay, it was…I'm not supposed to tell. I cannot."

Her mother stepped back and said, "Now, I want you to think about that. Who would ask you not to reveal their identity unless they have a reason to hide?"

"Mama, I gave my word. Both of you have taught me to honor my promises. 'Struth is, after I was partway there, too far to turn back, I realized I may have been too hasty in my decision. This man offered to assist me."

Her father's eyes widened. "And he didn't ask anything in return?"

"Just that I keep his identity a secret."

His sire ran a hand down his face. "Fine. I'll accept your answer for now, but I want to know everything that took place at Wingate. You discovered Randall is now the earl?"

"Aye." It suddenly struck her that he did not seem the least bit surprised. "Did you know. Papa? Why did you not tell us?"

"I knew, but I saw no purpose in telling you." He circled the desk and stood in front of her, crossing his arms. "Continue. Details, all of them."

"There is not much to tell. It was market day, and as soon as we arrived, I saw a couple of guards march Simone into the center of the courtyard. They tied her up and the housekeeper strutted around her with a strap, humiliating her in front of everyone for breaking a dish. To me it was our nightmare all over again. So I took action. I couldn't help myself. My first arrow struck the woman's arm and she dropped her strap. The second arrow hit one of the guards in his side, and then I threw a dagger and hit the second guard in his leg. He fell right to the ground. I grabbed Simone and we raced out of there."

"No one followed you?"

She stared at her feet. "Aye, we were chased by three men. I found a spot to hide and the two of us took the three of them out. They were the only ones who followed us. My partner believed them to be reivers. I heard them say they thought the earl would reward them for returning Simone and me. They weren't interested in the…" She halted, realizing how quickly she'd almost revealed Will's identity. "The man who was with me."

"And were you able to return to retrieve your arrows so Baines wouldn't be able to tell who'd shot them?"

Maggie fell into the chair, her hand coming up to her mouth before she glanced from her mother to her father. "Oh my word. I never thought…"

Her sire closed his eyes. "And now you know why one of us should have been with you. Randall Baines now knows our clan was responsible for the attack, and he is one of only twelve earls in England. Does that give you an idea of his power?"

"But he wasn't in residence," she said hurriedly, tripping over his words. "He left. He took Simone's sister somewhere. It shall be a while before he sees the arrows. Mayhap I can go back and retrieve them. Mama? Will you go with me?"

"Nay. The damage is done. Did you kill any of the first three?"

"Nay, I aimed to maim, just as you taught me. And the second group..."

Her father interrupted her with a sway of his hand in midair. "I'm not worried about reivers. I'm sure they were ready to suck coin out of whoever would willingly provide it. They weren't wearing the king's brooch, were they?"

"Nay, they were in various plaids."

"Reivers. If you're sure you only maimed the three in England, there should be no problem."

"The housekeeper wailed like a red fox in heat. My partner said the other two bore mild injuries."

"That may save us. If any of those three die, we could be in trouble."

Of course, that possibility had already occurred to her, but somehow it felt more real now that she was at home and not on the road. "What could he do?" she asked in a shaky voice.

Her sire answered her. "You were in England. Any crimes that happen in the Borderlands or nearby carry stiff penalties. The earl is the law in his land. He could hang you for murder if he chose to do so."

"What shall I do? We have to go save Beatris. Can we not leave at dawn?"

"Your mother and I will decide what's to be done once I speak with my brother and nephew. You will stay here, or I'll hang you myself, Maggie. Understood?" Her father glared at her.

"Aye, but can we not leave early on the morrow? Beatris…"

"We'll leave as soon as we have a plan. We'll make our decision by high noon on the morrow."

Her mother grasped her shoulders, massaging them gently. "Maggie, take care of Molly and Simone in the morning. I'll be conferring with your sire. Your sister needs to know you're hale. She was devastated when she learned you'd left on your own."

She just nodded, unable to remove four words from her mind.

Hang you for murder.

Her hands reflexively went up to guard her neck. What had she done?

CHAPTER NINE

WHEN MAGGIE GOT UP THE next morning, she made her way into the girls' chamber, pleased to see Simone and Brigid were giggling while Jennet tried to explain something to the pair of them.

"Simone, did you sleep well?"

She charged over to Maggie and gave her a hug. "Aye, 'twas the nicest bed I've ever been in, and the warmest, too. Are we leaving soon to find Beatris?"

The look of hope in the lass's face broke her heart. "Not this early. Why don't you wash up and break your fast with Brigid and Jennet. I'm going to tend my sister, and Papa is meeting with our lairds to form a plan. We'll leave this afternoon is my guess. Eat hearty as there is oft times little to eat on the road."

Simone blushed and stared at the floor.

"What's wrong, Simone?" She placed her finger under the girl's chin and tipped her head up so she could look into her eyes.

"Did you forget? Must I put that gown on again? It will remind me of the earl."

"Aye, I'm sorry, but I did forget. Jennet, please find two pairs of leggings and tunics for Simone. She'll be traveling with us and she needs to keep warm. And please bathe, all of you."

Brigid bounded out of bed. "I'll help you find clothing, Simone. Come see all the leggings we have. Our mama loves them."

Maggie nodded her thanks to her wee sister and left the

lassies, heading toward the chamber her sister shared with her husband. She knocked lightly, hoping not to disturb them if they were still asleep.

Tormod opened the door and ushered her inside. Molly peeked out from under the covers. "Good morn to you. Will you stay with me for a while? I'm not the best company right now, but I'd appreciate it."

"Of course." She turned to Tormod. "I'll help her get dressed if you have aught you need to do."

"I'd appreciate that. Your mother is busy this morn, and I'd like to join the scouting patrol for the archer who shot Molly. Someday we'll find something. I'll send some lads up with a tub. She wished to bathe this morn. Do you mind?"

"Nay, I'll help her."

Tormod gave Molly a final kiss, then nodded to Maggie before he left. His parting words before he closed the door were, "I should return when the sun is highest."

Maggie puttered around the small chamber after he left, putting things away, choosing Molly's clothing for the day. She pulled the furs back from the window, noting the gray skies but smiling at the crisp morning air. Winter was over, and the scent of spring hung in the air.

"Leave that back," Molly said in a small voice. "We need fresh air in here."

"That we do."

Two lads carried the tub inside along with a couple of large jugs of water, followed by the kitchen maids carrying steaming buckets of water. When they finished filling the tub, they closed the door behind them.

Molly heaved a sigh. "I just want to relax in the tub until the water goes cold. The warmth makes my ribs feel better. If you'll help me in, and give me the linen squares and the soap, I'll wash while you tell me all about your travels. I cannot believe you left on your own. What possessed you?"

Maggie helped her dear sister undress and climb into

the tub, then straightened the bed linens before she sat on a stool not far from the hearth. "Did Aunt Brenna tell you what you were dreaming before I left?"

"Aye. She said that I called you Randall, but I could hardly believe it. I don't remember any of it."

Maggie took a deep breath, knowing her sister was likely not happy with the decisions she'd made. "I could not handle seeing you in such a condition."

"What condition? Because I sprained my arm and broke some ribs? I've been lucky and had verra few injuries. 'Tis not so bad staying here and being fussed over by my husband. Do not pity me overly much." She closed her eyes and scrubbed her face.

She had to make her sister understand. Molly had always been her greatest supporter. If her parents disagreed with something she did, Molly would always help win them over. "Do you not remember the premonition you had after you fell? You dreamed about something dark, something near me." She noticed her sister struggling to turn in the water, so she hurried back to the tub, taking the soap and the linen to wash her back.

Molly sighed with pleasure, so she continued to rub her back for a moment, using soothing strokes. She then helped Molly tip her head back into the warm water so she could suds her hair with the soap. "I don't recall any of it. I'm so sorry. I do wish you'd stop worrying about me."

"But Molly…" How could she put her feelings into words? How could she properly express how much it had meant to her to be protected as a child? She rubbed her eye with the palm of her hand, hoping to erase any evidence of the blasted tears that kept decorating her face of late.

"But Molly what?" Her sister peered at her with an expression that went straight to her heart, squeezing it.

"You were all I had for so long, and you always protected me." She angrily swiped at her tears. Where were they coming from? She'd cried all over her mother the previous eve. She wished them away with a fury, but to no avail. They'd find a way to return. "I should have protected you, and I failed."

Molly gripped her hand to stand up in the tub. "The water has cooled off more quickly than I expected. Would you grab the large linen for me, please? Help me get dressed in front of the hearth?"

She jumped out of her spot and ran to do her sister's bidding.

"Protected me, Maggie? 'Tis no longer your job, 'tis Tormod's. Besides, how could you have stopped me from falling in the ravine?"

Maggie wrapped the linen around her and guided her over to the fire in the hearth. "Here, allow me to get your clothing and help you dress." She set the clothing near the fire to warm it. Once it was ready, she helped Molly with her leggings and then assisted her with the tunic, sliding it over her injured arm carefully before pulling it down. "I'll fix your hair for you, help you with your boots, and then run to the kitchens to fetch some food for you…"

Molly grabbed her hand and pulled her close. "Maggie? What is it? Why are you acting like this? None of this was your fault, and it was not your fault I called Baines's name out in the middle of the night. Why are you taking all the blame on your shoulders?"

"Because…because…" Saints above, but she was losing all control. Tears flooded down her cheeks and she did her best to control her sobs and her hitching breath. "Molly, you protected me all those years. You think I didn't know every time you begged Baines's housekeeper to take my punishment? You think I didn't see the blood on your clothing after a whipping? That I didn't hear you crying in the middle of the night? I tried so hard not to make a mistake or spill anything, but it still kept happening. The beatings that you endured were almost all my fault, and I owe you…" Her breathing hitched. "And I should take care of you now, and I didn't…and…"

Maggie stared into her sister's beautiful eyes, watching the tears as they formed and fell down her rosy cheeks. "Maggie, nay…"

"Aye, my fault. I had to go after him, make him pay. After all these years, that bastard still haunts you, and when I saw that woman beating Simone, something snapped inside me…and I shouldn't have…but…but…Papa says the earl could have me hung for murder…if they died…or…"

"Hush, Maggie."

Her sister tugged her gently until her head fell onto her shoulder, and she finally allowed herself to release all the tears that had been pricking at her eyes. Oh, how she loved her sister.

Molly's voice soothed her just as it always had when they were young. "Now, you listen to me. None of those lashings hurt as much as you thought they did, and you were too young. You were a wee lassie when he wished to use a switch on you the first time, and I'd not allow such a thing to happen to my sister. I'd do the same all over again. He couldn't destroy *us*, that was all what mattered to me. Promise me you'll think no more on this. I do not hold it against you at all, and I have verra few scars."

Maggie closed her eyes and thought of all her sister had said. Was she right? Even a small part of it?

Molly continued, still holding her tight, "You and I survived. You probably do not recall the wee lassie that was your age who died from her punishments. You didn't know because they hid it, but I cared for her until the day she succumbed." She pulled back and lifted her gaze up to hers. "I could not allow that to happen to you. Here is what I wish you to remember about our time with him. We survived. Together. As much as he or his helpers tried to break us apart, they could not. We survived because Gwyneth and Logan Ramsay discovered his cruelty and put an end to it. They gave us a home and became our parents."

Despite her hitching breath, Maggie managed to nod at her sister. "But he's still doing it to others. To Simone, to Beatris…"

"And now we are in a position to put an end to his habit of torturing children. Mama and Papa will see to it, but you have to promise me you'll never put yourself at risk again. 'Twas dangerous running off on your own like that. We can do this together, well, I may not travel with you, but there are so many lads and lasses in the clan eager to help you. This time we'll do it right."

But she hadn't been alone. Will had been with her, and he'd made her feel safe. Her next sentence came out in a flurry of words. "Molly, I met someone and I like him."

Her sister gasped. "You did? Tell me everything." She moved over to a chair and patted the chair next to her. It was a balm to Maggie's soul that she moved quickly and without apparent pain. "Tell me. Who is he?"

"I cannot. I swore not to reveal his identity, but he's so handsome."

Her sister clapped her hands and the two of them collapsed into a fit of giggles. "Tell me more," Molly said through her laughter.

"His hair is dark, and his eyes are the strangest mixture of blue and green. He's tall and strong, yet gentle."

Molly's eyes widened, and her voice came out in a low squeal. "He kissed you? He must have or you would not have called him gentle."

Maggie nodded, blushing as her thoughts went to Will and his warm lips and how good he'd tasted.

"Well, I'll not push you to tell me who he is so long as you promise to introduce us as soon as you are able."

Maggie grasped her sister's hands. "I will, I promise. I hope to see him again when we ride off to find Baines."

Aye, he'd said he could not risk meeting anyone else from

her clan, but surely the kiss had changed things between them. Whatever he was running from, she wished to help him.

"And you must promise me something else, or I'll never sleep another night. Promise me you'll not attack Randall Baines alone, whatever happens. He could cause so much trouble now that he has the power of Wingate behind him. Go rescue the lassie, aye, but leave him be and let Papa deal with him."

Maggie didn't know what to say. Could she do what her sister asked? Her mind filled with images of Simone being whipped, of Molly crying in her sleep, of Molly swinging at her and calling her Randall. She had to be brutally honest. "I'm not certain I can make that promise."

Molly reached out and grabbed her hand. "Please, Maggie. I could not bear to be sitting here worrying about what might happen to you. Even if you have not committed murder, he could see you imprisoned in an English gaol. When would I ever see you again?"

Maggie stopped, her mind going over her sister's comment. One of the greatest fears she'd always had was imprisonment. What if that happened? What if someone brought one of her arrows to the earl? What if he remembered her from their time in Edinburgh? What if he sent his marshal out in search of her to bring her to justice?

There would be no fairness to whatever he decided. If he imprisoned her, she'd wish she were dead within a sennight.

But if he were dead...

"I'm sorry, Molly. I cannot make that promise."

Molly stood from her chair with difficulty. "You must. Please. You are my dearest sister and the thought of you or anyone I love being imprisoned in England makes me quite ill. Please, Maggie."

Maggie stared at her sister and shook her head slowly. "I'm so sorry..."

She turned and ran out of the room—and then kept running, down the stairs and out the doorway of the great hall. She had to get away but where? How could one man ruin so many lives from such a long distance? If she saw the bastard, she'd cut him down for sure.

She made her way to the stables, pleased she didn't run into her mother or sire or her brother. Without thinking, she found and mounted her favorite horse, then dashed through the gates with the wind in her unbraided hair.

Imprisoned? Hung for murder? What was this nonsense?

She took off with no idea where she was headed. She just had to get away.

CHAPTER TEN

WILL LEFT HIS HORSE AND headed closer to Ramsay Castle. He'd seen the patrols out earlier, presumably searching for the man who'd attacked Molly. Not daring to bring his horse any closer, he'd tied him up and run through the woods until he found the spot that gave him the best possible view of the castle. He'd left the puppy with his grandsire as company.

He wasn't in the tree for long before a horse came barreling out the gates at a frantic pace. Long before he caught sight of her face, he knew it could only be Maggie.

She rode her horse like they were one, her body suspended low across the beast, as she raced across the meadow and headed straight for the path in the woods, her brown hair free and waving wildly in the wind as she traveled. He waited until she was close before letting out a piercing whistle, hoping she would hear him. She slowed her horse, searching the area for the source of the sound.

He jumped down from the tree and ran straight toward her. "Maggie!" He hoped she would recognize his voice and not be afraid of him. Once he came to a clearing, he could see her a bit better in the distance. He waved and called out to her. "Maggie, what's wrong?"

To his surprise she jumped down from her horse and headed toward him, running as fast as she could. At the last minute, he held his arms out, only because he thought he noticed the tears in her eyes. God's teeth, but he'd do aught he could to comfort her. She looked so beautiful, so sad…

She flew into his arms and he held her tight. "What's

wrong?" he repeated.

Instead of answering him, she surprised him even more by kissing him hard on the lips, teasing him with her tongue until they dueled with each other in a passionate frenzy the likes of which he'd never experienced before. The sensation of her body pressed against his fueled him even more until he knew there was no way he could hide his reaction to her.

Fortunately, it did not scare her at all this time. She pulled back for a second to stare at him, and the passion in her eyes went straight to his cock, so he kissed her again, plundering her mouth until they both were panting as if in a race against time. He tasted every bit of her, angling his mouth over hers as they eagerly shared this part of themselves with the other. He ran his hands down her back and her bottom, cupping her softness and pulling her close, so close he swore he could feel the heat coming from her. Hell but he wanted this moment to go on forever. He pulled away enough to kiss a trail to her ear, teasing her with his tongue as he moved his way down her neck. To his astonishment, her passion matched his own. Her hands roamed all over his body, squeezing him and teasing him everywhere until she tugged on his tunic and found her way up his chest, her fingertips brushing across his nipples.

He pulled away, his grandsire's warning fresh in him mind. "Maggie, I want you more than I've ever wanted any woman, but not here. 'Tis not right."

She kissed him, small feathery kisses on his cheek and the scruff of his beard across his chin. "Please, when I'm with you, I forget. Everything washes away, all my worries, my fears, everything. I need you, Will."

He stopped her advances to cup her face. "What happened? Tell me." He could see how she fought the tears in her eyes.

She moved away from him and began to pace, but he didn't want any distance between them. Not yet. *Not ever*, a voice in his head whispered. He grasped her hand and sat down on the ground, tugging her onto his lap. She just closed her eyes and crumpled against him, her head resting on his shoulder.

"Tell me everything," he whispered, wrapping his arms around her.

"Papa is furious that I left without him and even more so that I went to England alone. I told him about saving Simone and the first thing he asked was whether we retrieved our arrows, which we didn't. Now he's concerned that Baines will recognize our colors and come after us. Papa said if anyone died, the earl could hang me for murder."

"You mean hang us, do you not? I was there, too."

She cupped his face and stared into his eyes. "Do you think we killed any of them? I aimed only to maim. I'm certain I hit the woman in her shoulder. She was still moving."

"And cursing you out. 'Tis why the other two came to her assistance. You hit one in the side and the other in the leg. Both were still yelling when you grabbed Simone. 'Tis the last thing I remember. Those men did not die from the wounds we inflicted. And the fools that followed us were not the king's men. They were lowlifes hoping to profit from the situation. Believe me, no one will miss them."

"He said he was not worried about the reivers. But the ones on English soil…what if they succumbed to their wounds?"

"There is no sense worrying about something you cannot change. I was with you, so whatever you are accused of, they will do the same with me." His thumb brushed across her cheek in a rhythm he hoped would calm her. Saints above, but he feared he would do most anything for this woman on his lap.

"And then Molly said they might put me in an English gaol." She leaned her forehead against his and whispered, "Will, if that ever happened, I'd never survive. I have such a fear of small places, and besides, Baines would use it as an excuse to torture me. And I must go after Beatris."

He cupped her face and gazed into her eyes. "Whatever happens, you know your sire will get you out. And if he does not, then I will."

She reached up to cover his hand with her own. "He's so upset with me. I don't know…"

"Do not be foolish. Everyone knows Logan Ramsay would do aught he could to save his children."

"But I'm adopted."

"That means naught to him, and I think you know that. He's a most fair man. You must trust him. What about Beatris? Will your sire go after Baines?"

"He's in the solar strategizing with our laird, Torrian, and my uncle Quade. My sire said he would help, but he's not moving fast enough to suit me. If he doesn't act soon, I'll have to leave alone again, no matter what he says. I can't abide the thought of aught happening to those lasses. Will you go with me? We could go by ourselves and leave everyone behind." Her fingers moved up to his face and she played with the scruff of his beard, his lips, everything she could find until he chuckled.

"I know you are doing that without thinking, but it tickles. I like you verra much, Maggie."

"I like you, too." She sighed as if she never wished to leave him. "Will, what shall we do?"

He reached for her distracting fingers and cocooned them inside his own, sighing deeply. "I don't think you'll like my answer, but we cannot go alone."

She tugged her hand away with a snap. "Why not? I thought you would agree with me."

He clasped her hand again, not allowing her to pull away from him. He enjoyed their closeness too much. "How will you even know who Beatris is if you find her?" He uncovered her hand and brought each of her fingertips up to his lips, kissing each one with a tenderness he hoped would calm her. He could feel the wild beating of her heart and could see every time a new thought entered her mind.

"Saints above, you're right. We must take Simone."

"And…" He wanted her to come to the right conclusion on her own.

"And we cannot risk aught happening to her. You're right. We should wait to see what my parents have decided."

"Good. I don't think they will wait. From what Gavin and Gregor have told me, they take action quickly, but they don't go anywhere without a plan."

She rested her head back on his shoulder. "What you say is true. We'll wait. I wish you would come to the hall with me."

"I cannot."

"When will you tell me why?"

"In time. You must go back now and find out your sire's plan. Know that I'll follow your group out and stay as close as I dare. Your sire is a hell of a scout, and if I'm lucky, Gavin and Gregor will travel with you. They would never betray me."

She sat up and kissed him quickly. "I better go back. I hope we'll be moving soon. Please come with us."

"Naught could keep me away. I'll be waiting, and never fear, I'll always be behind you somewhere."

She hurried away, but he called after her, "I meant what I said, lass."

She halted, giving him a confused look.

"If anyone ever locks you up, I'll get you out."

———◆———

MAGGIE HURRIED BACK TO THE castle, surprised to see her sire heading toward the stables. As soon as he saw her, he shouted to her, "Get your things ready and get Simone. We're heading out within the hour. The next time you see your boyfriend, tell him he may come along, but he's to stay out of sight."

Maggie stopped in her tracks, her face turning a flaming red. She'd been caught by her father.

He leaned over and kissed her cheek, whispering, "Your brother and cousin are not as good at keeping secrets as you are. I've known about Will's training with Gavin and Gregor for some time now. I'm not surprised he finds you more interesting, but if he ever oversteps, I'll be there to castrate him. Give him my warning."

"Papa, why must he hide?"

"He hasn't told you?"

"Nay." Her hands perched on her hips, waiting for him to give her the answer to her question.

"He'll tell you when he's ready."

"You don't know either."

He rolled his eyes with a smirk. "And I don't know he's out there waiting for you, and I'm not a spy for the Scottish Crown either. Give me a little credit, lass. I don't need to wait to be told things to know them." He spun on his heel, heading toward the stables, chuckling.

She shouted to his back. "But Papa, do you like him?"

He stopped to turn back to her. "I've never met the lad, only heard about him and watched him from afar. He was smart enough to follow you when you let your emotions drive you from the keep, so I suppose I'll have to thank him for that someday." Then he smiled and winked at her. "I didn't expect to hear a Falconer act like a dove, but now that you two are cooing at each other, I hope he continues to act honorably. He needs to stay alert."

Her mother came along and patted her shoulder as she passed her. "You lassies will never learn, will you? Your sire is everywhere. Go ready yourself and Simone. We need to find Beatris."

She opened her mouth to give her mother a fast retort, but nothing came out. Saints above, they all knew she'd gone off with Will.

Focus, Maggie.

Will *was* too distracting.

She forced him out of her mind and raced up the steps to the great hall. As soon as she opened the door, she stopped abruptly because Simone already stood there in front of her, satchel in hand, awaiting her arrival.

"Are we ready? Your mama says we're going for Beatris." A lone tear fell down and landed with a plop on her tunic. "We'll find her, won't we, my lady?"

She bent down so she was at her height. "Call me Maggie, Simone. We'll be working together, so we must be able to communicate quickly. You should address my mother and my aunts as such, but not me." She brushed the next tear away. "Aye, we'll find her. My sire is the best tracker in all the land, and my mother is the best archer. Hopefully, we'll have your sister back here in a few days."

"May we remain here after you find her? I do not wish to go back to England."

"Aye, you may stay here. I'm sure my clan will welcome you, though I've not had the time to ask. Do not worry. My mother and sire will open their arms to you. Now you must get tough and stay focused. Are you ready?"

Simone lifted her chin. "I'm ready. And if you wish, I can get through spaces a big person cannot. I can also pretend to be a lad if you need me to be."

"What a wonderful idea. I must pack my own satchel, but I promise to return quickly. Go to the kitchens and pack a few oatcakes or whatever you can fit in your satchel. Pack what Beatris will eat. I'm sure she'll be hungry when we find her."

She had to smile at how quickly Simone spun around to follow her instructions, dodging between the trestle tables to find her way to the kitchens in the back.

How she prayed she was right. They had to find Beatris. She owed it to Simone and to Molly. Deep down, she also owed it to herself.

It could be the only way she'd be able to overcome the dark truths of her past.

CHAPTER ELEVEN

———◆———

RANDALL BAINES OPENED THE DOOR to the great hall, furious he'd been delayed by his human cargo. "What is it now, Eda?"

The servant waved to him from a side door, indicating that he should follow her. Hell, but he didn't like anyone thinking they could give him orders. "You better have a good reason for calling me into this chamber, or I'll see your arse whipped." He had too many things to worry about at the moment.

As soon as he stepped inside the chamber, he knew what she wanted.

"Shite. What happened?" He glanced at the state of the chamber. Various body fluids had been spilled over different parts of the floor. He brought his hand up to his nose as if he could stop the smell from assaulting the hair in his nostrils.

"That wee one is sick. You'll not get her there in time. No one would buy her." She pointed to the pallet in the corner where one of the lasses lay, her eyes closed.

"She looks dead."

"She's close to it. You cannot take her. I know not what makes her heave. All of us could catch it. We must send her back to England."

"Nay." He shook his head before he made his way back out the door, gagging. "Leave her here. She'll never survive the trip back to England. She'll die soon. We'll bury her when we come back through. I'm not touching her now, and neither will I send anyone else in to deal with her. It could be a death sentence. Get the other two ready and pack your things. We're leaving soon. We have to meet the men at the firth in one hour. I won't be delayed."

She followed him out into the hall. "You'll just leave a wee bairn here to die? Even I'm not that cold."

"You cannot stay with her. I need you to handle the other two. The ship will be waiting for us. We must leave now."

He hurried toward the door of the keep, anxious to breathe in fresh air. The entire hall would stink soon enough. He sure as hell did not want whatever ailed the wee lass. As soon as he stepped outside, two guards hurried toward him. "What is it?" he asked Aldus Bullard, one of his best guards.

"We return with Captain Granville. He says we're searching for any Ramsays along the way."

"True. And a bonus to anyone who brings me a Ramsay, no matter what their age."

Aldus smiled. "I'll be sure to mention that to my brother. He'll find one for you, right enough."

"Then tell him if he finds one in less than a sennight and brings him or her here before I return from the firth, I'll double the payment.

Aldus grinned, "Aye, my lord. Consider it done. My brother and I will find one for you. Which one would you like?"

Baines thought for a moment, almost ready to say it didn't matter, but then an image of a wee lass popped into his head. The girl had caused him plenty of trouble with King Alexander all those years ago.

With a grin and a feeling of elation, he said, "Molly. That's the one I want. Bring her to me. I hear she's the best archer they have now."

CHAPTER TWELVE

M AGGIE'S HANDS GREW CLAMMY WHEN they reached Edinburgh. The entire city was surrounded by a wall, and the royal castle, perched above all else on a rock outcropping, had its own curtain wall. They traveled with more men than they usually did, mostly because Maggie's sire wanted warriors in case he had to take Baines's men down at his estate.

"How far from here, Papa?"

He led them to a clearing outside the city, motioning for the guards to patrol while he addressed the rest of their group. Maggie dismounted and helped Simone down. They clustered together under a tree—her mother and father, Gavin and Gregor, and one guard who would relay instructions to the others.

A rustling behind them caused three swords to unsheathe in a flash, but a voice called out, "'Tis only me, Will. I'm here to help."

To her surprise and utter delight, Will emerged from the woods and strode toward them, his gaze directed at her sire, his hands raised in front of him to show he had no weapons. "I'm on your side."

Dressed all in black, he stood in the center of the group and seemed taller and broader than any of them. Her heart skipped a beat as she waited to see how her sire would respond to his presence. His bow was over his shoulder and he had a sword sheathed on his back. Her desire to reach out for his hand was almost overwhelming. "I was with Maggie when she saved Simone. I'd like to continue to help. This bastard deserves to be taken down."

Simone ran to him and threw her arms around his waist. Maggie wished she dared to do the same, but she decided to remain aloof toward Will in front of her family. If she did what she wished to do, she'd spend the next several minutes doing naught but enjoying his presence—his clean scent, the scruff of his dark beard, his strong jawline, and those turquoise eyes that pulled her in every time. For now, she was satisfied with just a glimpse of his lips and his broad chest...

"Maggie!"

She jerked her head around to look at her sire, doing her best to ignore the smirk on her mother's face.

"Are you with us? Should I allow him along or will he prove to be too distracting for you?"

"Nay, of course not. Carry on." She did her best to hide her blush, but the others were all staring at her, which only served to deepen the color on her cheeks.

"I'm sending Gavin and Gregor down that street first," Logan said. "We shall wait at the end. Will, do you wish to go with them?"

"Aye."

"Leave your bows. You'll need your swords ready in case you find anyone inside. We'll be in position to shoot if anyone runs."

"What about me?" Simone asked.

"Simone, we'll need you to identify your sister, but first we must assess the situation. 'Tis more of a manor home than 'tis a castle, so I don't expect many men to be here. In fact, you three head out now and we'll follow. Gavin, stay calm and keep control of yourself."

Gavin and Gregor mounted their horses and waited for Will to return with his horse before heading out. She caught a quick wink from Will as he passed them again—a small gesture that sent such a burning wave of heat through her body that she quickly turned away from him. Fortunately, her parents hadn't noticed since they were now talking with three Ramsay guards who'd returned from patrolling.

Her sire led the way a short time after the others left. They traveled at a canter into Edinburgh and across town to Baines castle. Maggie was not particularly fond of Edinburgh because it held many bad memories for her, but she had a purpose today.

A quarter of an hour later, they found their way to the end of the street, surprised to see Gregor headed straight toward them.

"There's no one there, Uncle Logan. I've never seen a castle deserted like that."

Simone let out a cry as Will and Gavin reached their side. "No servants, no evidence of anyone around," Gavin agreed. "There's no one in the hall, and the stables and kitchens are completely empty."

"Did you search the entire place?" Maggie asked.

"Nay, we did not go upstairs, just the main floor," Gavin said. "There's no need."

Simone's tears prompted Maggie to make her move. "Papa, I aim to do a proper search. There's too much at risk to be hasty."

"I'll go with her," her mother said. "Simone and Will can come with us."

Leaving their horses near the street, they made their way in through the front door. Since there was no one at the gates, they weren't worried about encountering anyone else. Will headed up the stairs, and Maggie moved to follow him with Simone, but her mother gave Simone a pointed look and said, "You stay here. I'll go with him. Allow him to make sure none of Baines's men are hiding up there first."

After the two left, Simone pointed to a chamber at the end of the hall. "There. We were here once, and I think we slept in a chamber over there. All of us."

Maggie clutched Simone's hand and made her way to the end of the hall. A door was hidden behind a large tapestry, barely visible to anyone entering the hall. She opened it slowly, noticing the strong odor emanating from the chamber as soon as it was open to the hall. Something told her to continue inside despite the closeness and the strong odor.

"Beatris!" Simone pointed to the small unmoving form on the farthest pallet. She ran to her sister's side and knelt there, calling her name as she reached for her hand. "Beatris, wake up. It's me, Simone. Please wake up."

Maggie didn't know if the lassie was dead or alive. Afraid to find out for sure, she had to propel herself forward, fear of the worst holding her back. What if they'd arrived too late? What if she was already dead or so near death that they'd never revive her? What if she carried the fever? She took a few steps closer and gazed down at the lass.

She was a beautiful girl, with porcelain skin and brown hair that might have been a caramel blonde if it had been washed recently. The tone of her skin was dry and waxy, one of the first things Maggie noticed because it was an unnatural cast for certain. Her eyes were closed and she was motionless. Maggie thought she saw a slight rise of the lassie's chest, but she wasn't certain. She lay in filth. It was clear the poor thing had vomited recently…and equally clear she'd been left to her fate.

The door opened and she spun around, her hand going to her dagger, but it was only her mother. "There's no one up there," she said as her gaze moved to Beatris and Simone, now crying.

Her mother moved in closer and whispered in Maggie's ear, "Is it too late?"

She shook her head. "I don't think so. She still breathes."

Her mother stepped around her and knelt next to the pallet. "Oh, sweet lassie." She caressed Beatris's cheek, but the girl did not respond. "She's still alive." She patted Simone's hand in comfort and then glanced over her shoulder at Maggie. "Did Simone bring extra clothing?"

Maggie nodded. "I think so."

"We need to get her out of these clothes and off that filthy pallet."

How she adored her mother. Would she ever learn to act so quickly and decisively?

Simone continued to call her sister's name while Maggie and Gwyneth worked to get the wee lass out of her clothes. They left her chemise on but tossed the soiled dress to the floor. When Will entered the room, Maggie told him to get Simone's satchel form the back of her horse.

He asked nary a question, but the look in his eyes before he left the room attested that he understood the gravity of the situation. Simone turned to Maggie's mother, tears tracking down her cheeks. "Is she dead? Is my sister dead?"

Maggie placed her ear against the lassie's chest. "Her heart still beats."

"But she needs treatment quickly," Gwyneth whispered. "You dress her, Maggie, while I go speak with your sire." She picked the wee one up and settled her on Maggie's lap, though the lassie was limp as a worn rag.

Moments later, Will rushed in with the satchel. Simone helped Maggie get the fresh tunic over Beatris' slight shoulders and the leggings on her spindly limbs. The wee lassie was impossibly thin. "She's too cold," Maggie whispered.

"What will we do now?" Simone asked. "We have to save her. She never ate much at Baines's castle. She hated the food there. She would only drink goat's milk, but they rarely had it."

"Give her to me," Will said. "My body will warm her more than yours." He picked her up and gently cocooned her against his chest, carrying her out of the hall and into the fresh air, though it was a little cool outside.

Her father stared at Will and said, "Well?"

Maggie had no idea what that meant. It was as if he expected Will to handle the situation on his own. "Papa?"

Will didn't hesitate to respond. "I'll take her to my grandsire. He's a healer. He lives about an hour away."

"Move your arse, MacLerie. Do what you must. Take Gavin and Gregor with you. Simone and Maggie, too. Gwynie and I are going after Baines. I don't know what he's about, but it can't be good."

W ILL HELD THE LASS IN front of him. Gwyneth had tied her to him with an extra plaid to keep her safely attached to him while he rode. He didn't know what to think. The lassie was on death's door, but mayhap his mother was watching from above and would guide them in the right direction. He'd placed his hand on her chest, hoping some magic would come through and heal her, but to no avail. His mother's gift wasn't his.

His grandsire could help her for sure, but only if he managed to keep the poor lassie alive until then.

As soon as they arrived, he rushed inside with the child, leaving Gavin and Gregor to help Simone and Maggie. There was not a minute to waste.

"Grandpapa, I'm here with the Ramsays. You must heal the lassie." He placed the tiny bairn on the bed while his grandsire followed him.

"Where is she hurt?"

"I don't know. She's been heaving, but we found her like this. There's no blood."

"Does she have the fever?" He placed the back of his hand against her cheek and then her neck.

"Nay, she's too cold. What can we do?"

"Feed her, first. She looks like she's been starved. She must be thirsty, too. Grab the pitcher over there. I have fresh goat's milk. We'll try that." He pointed to the urn on his table, and Will hurried to get it, Maggie and Simone were just coming inside with the lads behind them.

"Please save my sister," Simone cried and grabbed Beatris's hand. "Beatris? Beatris? Please wake up."

"How old is she, lass?" Will asked.

"She's just five summers, but they make her work like she's ten summers like me."

Will's grandsire said, "I'm too old to kneel next to her." He pointed to Maggie and said, "Kneel and give her this goat's milk. But you must be careful because she's not awake enough to swallow. I hope she will, but we'll tip her head to the side a wee bit so it will slowly roll down her throat."

Maggie did as he instructed, feeding the bairn wee portions of the milk, but she let out a squeal when the lass began to choke. "I'm sorry, I'm so sorry."

Will's grandsire patted her arm. "Nay, that's a good sign. Let her cough."

Beatris coughed three more times. Her lids popped up and she stared at Maggie. Simone, whose eyes had gone huge, grasped her shoulder and said, "Beatris? It's me. Say something, please."

"Simone?" Her voice came out in a dry crack, and she pointed to the goblet Maggie held. "More, please?"

"Sit her up, Maggie," Will said. "Put her on your lap, then hold the goblet for her. Let her take it at her own pace."

The lassie took another sip, and then the strangest thing happened. Beatris began to cry but she shed no tears. She alternated between two words—"more" and "Simone." Maggie had never seen anyone cry dry tears before. It was an oddity that caused her heart to break, the sound quite unnerving.

Once Beatris finished the goblet, Will's grandsire said, "I think we'll let that settle in her belly for a bit and wash her up. Once she's clean, we'll try to feed her some broth."

Will retrieved the soap and linen squares while Gavin and Gregor found a small tub and filled it with water.

Once they finished, Will's grandsire pointed to the door. "Let's go outside, lads, eh?" As soon as they were gathered outside the house, he pointed to the two Ramsay lads and asked, "Can you hunt with those bows? How about getting a couple of rabbits for us to roast?"

The lads nodded, pleased to do one of their favorite things. Both were exceptional hunters.

Will watched them leave, and once they were gone, he turned to his grandsire and said, "It did not work. For once, I hoped I would have Mama's power, but it did not work."

"You're fooling yourself if you think it means you're no healer. Healing powers can only do so much. There must be some illness or injury there that needs fixing. This child has been starved to death. Healing powers cannot feed a child. All you can do is get her heart to continue a while longer. 'Tis the same reason we cannot save the elderly. Once 'tis gone, 'tis gone. A healer cannot make a brand new heart."

"I don't understand. I thought a healer could heal anyone. The power makes choices?" His grandfather made no sense sometimes. He wondered if his mind was going.

"Do not look at me as though I'm daft. Just because you're a young'un doesn't mean I'm ready to be put out in the forest to die. Think on it, lad. What about the boy your mother healed?"

"He took an arrow in the belly. She healed him. What more is there to it?"

"She healed him because the arrow had sliced his insides. Your mother could reattach whatever had been ripped open. If a bone broke, she could put it back together. If a vessel was cut, she could reattach it with the heat of her hand. You can heal from the inside, not the outside. 'Tis what I've been trying to tell you."

"Nay, I cannot heal anyone at all. Mama did not think I had the skill. Why must you continue to bring it up?"

"I'm just hopeful, lad. The world needs more healers.

Did you feel aught when you touched the lass?"

"How would I know?" Will asked. In truth, he'd always wondered if he did have her gift. She'd always hoped he would develop it someday. Most days he looked upon the possibility as a curse, but he would have liked to heal the bairn.

"Heat. Your mother would feel heat come down her arm. She would place her hand over the part that needed healing."

"Nay," he said with a sigh. "I felt nothing. So there's truly naught wrong with her except a lack of food and drink?"

"Aye. Lacking fluid will kill a person faster than not eating. You can go days without food, but a failure to drink can bring quick death. The question is why? Why would someone starve the wee lass?"

"It was clear she'd been spewing when we found her on the pallet. No one had bothered to clean it up. It would make me sick to lie near it. No wonder she worsened."

"Where did you find her?"

"She was at Randall Baines's estate in Edinburgh, but she'd been left behind all on her own. What cruelty is that to leave a child alone to die?"

His grandsire sighed and closed his eyes. "This earl is going to be naught but trouble. I asked around about him in the village as I promised I would. He and his friends are into some dirty business, they are. And being an earl, 'twill be hard to stop him. He's as slippery as the grease from a drove of piglets."

CHAPTER THIRTEEN

———

R ANDALL BAINES PACED NEAR THE firth. He'd brought everyone with him because he didn't wish to travel without protection, and he was uneasy about someone going for help for the girl. He didn't keep a large staff at his Edinburgh estate anyway, so it was no trouble to bring everyone along. He'd sent some out patrolling so they wouldn't be witness to his exchange. The usual cargo wasn't a worry, but the human cargo could prove more complicated. They needed to be careful about who they trusted.

The child they'd left behind would die, and then she would no longer be his problem. When they returned, his men would bury her. At least she'd proven valuable as a lesson—slightly older girls made for more reliable cargo.

Randall knew he was crossing a line, but he needed a ready source of coin. What could it hurt to sell a few? Their own parents didn't want them, so who would care?

It took considerable coin to keep his castles intact. The one his sire had built in Edinburgh was small and uncomfortable, but it had its uses as a base for getting his cargo to and from the Firth of Forth. Though he had no desire to establish a life in the land of the savages, it was much better to do his business here than risk getting caught in London.

While he and his sire had worked in the export business together, gathering and selling stolen goods, the profits had been steady though not spectacular. After the old earl's death, he'd been approached about something that could make him a real fortune. He'd have enough money to build a fine castle in London and establish the kind of lifestyle he deserved.

But he also knew he was taking a risk. If he got caught by the wrong people, he could lose everything. His title would protect him, yes, but only so far.

His marshal came up behind him. "How much longer before the ship arrives? It's not easy keeping those girls quiet. Eda had to put them to sleep with some concoction." He paused and gave him a significant look. "I worry about her, Wingate. She doesn't take to the work."

Baines ran a hand through his hair. "I know, but I offered her a good payment. She'll keep her mouth shut if she wishes to stay with me. She doesn't like the lash any more than the wee ones do."

"How many sales of this kind of cargo are you planning after this?"

"Not sure." He moved over to the edge of the water, thinking he heard something, but in the dark of the night, it was hard to see anyone. How the hell a ship could maneuver in this area was beyond him.

"Just exactly what are you selling besides the two girls?"

"He's sending another ship in a fortnight for one more journey east. I promised him five in the next load."

"And what else?"

"More wool, some metal, but he offered me the most money for whisky. I have to find a source here in Scotland. You know how the savages like to hide their best supply. I need to uncover one. You and I will focus on that. We'll find a few more wee ones, and while we're at it, we'll steal some whisky. A load of whisky and children will pay enough for me to start building a new castle in London."

Marshal deVere chuckled. "I wish it were so easy. How can you promise something you're not certain you'll be able to find?"

What right did his marshal have to question him? Baines lost his composure in an instant. "Do not ever question me.

I've been taking young girls from their homes in England for years. You'd be surprised how many parents are anxious to get rid of the extra mouths to feed. I promise to give their children fine lives in a noble household and they hand them over with a smile."

"And the whisky?" deVere pressed. "You'll have to fight Highland savages for it."

"I'll find a way. Perhaps I'll blackmail Logan Ramsay. He's bound to have tons of it and now that I have evidence of his involvement in the murders at Wingate, I'll be able to negotiate."

"What murders? Those arrows didn't kill anyone. You have two injured men and a whining housekeeper."

"He doesn't know that, does he? Once I tell our king it was murder, he'll have to negotiate. They'll never know the truth. If they dare come near my estate, I'll throw the Wild Falconer and the Ramsay girl in the gaol. See how they like that. Logan will pay us in whisky to get her out. There's always a way."

"I hope you know what you're doing, my lord." DeVere walked back to the area where the cargo was well hidden.

He wiped the sweat from his brow. DeVere couldn't be more right.

One mistake and *he* could be hung.

———◆———

MAGGIE FOUGHT TEARS AS SHE watched Simone fuss over her sister. The only thing she could do to get Beatris to respond was to put the puppy on her lap. Then her eyes would open and she'd smile, petting him with glee. Unfortunately, the glee turned to exhaustion, and her eyes would close again. Memories of the time she and her sister had spent in the care of Randall Baines surfaced and tore her heart out, especially when she thought of how helpless Molly was at present.

The door opened and Will entered the cottage. He

walked to her side and squeezed her hand, a simple gesture that she returned. Somehow his touch comforted
her rather than alarmed her. "How is she?" he asked in an
undertone.

"About the same."

"I'll get some broth for her." He moved to the hearth
and scooped some broth in a bowl from the mutton soup
steeping in the large pot over the fire. "Here. See if she'll
try this."

Maggie fed the bairn carefully, making sure the broth
wasn't too hot before giving it to her. Once the wee one
took her first swallow, she nodded and whispered, "More,
please?"

Simone glanced from Will to Maggie. "She'll be fine in
another day or two, won't she? You won't make us return
to Castle Wingate, will you? I like Scotland. We'll be good
helpers at the keep."

Maggie said, "Aye, 'tis as I said. We'll never send you back
to England. As soon as Beatris is able to make the journey,
we'll return to Ramsay Castle."

After Beatris took a few more sips, she placed her wee
hand on Maggie's and asked, "Where are the other girls?"

"Other girls?" Maggie replied. "You were alone when
we found you."

She shook her head, her forehead furrowed in agitation.
"No. Lord Baines took all three of us. Me and Geva and
Emma. Where did they go?"

Will's grandsire stepped inside the door, moving over to
listen to the conversation. Maggie stared at Will, hoping he
would approve of her plan. "We must go after them."

"Mayhap your mother and father have found them."

"Aye, but what if they haven't? They have no idea they
have to search for two lasses. Simone, do you know how
old they are?"

"Yes, Geva is seven and Emma is six. They're sisters."

Beatris glanced at Will and added, "They're my friends."

She gave him a wee smile before taking another sip of the broth. "I'm five and Emma is six and Geva is seven. Five, six, seven," she said, her face lit up with pride at her skill. "But where are they?" Her smile vanished in an instant.

Maggie's heart beat hard in her chest as she waited for Will's answer. Finally, he looked at his grandsire and said, "Maggie and I will go after the other girls, hopefully find her parents for assistance. Can you handle the wee lassies for a bit? If we see Gavin and Gregor…"

The door burst open. "We're here. Left a pheasant that needs to be plucked outside. What are you planning?" Gavin asked.

"There were two lassies with Beatris. We're going after them. Mama and Papa don't know they're with Baines, and we need to make sure they're not left behind," Maggie said, setting Beatris down in a chair near the hearth.

"Where are we going?" Gregor asked.

Will's grandsire sighed, then said, "I know where you need to go. That's what I discovered on my visit to the village. There's a cargo ship coming up the firth, but 'tis coming in on the point, not the docks. No one knows why, but I can easily guess. Someone's stealing and selling. The dirty earl, it would seem."

Will grinned. "I know exactly where that is. Thanks, Grandpapa." He turned to Gavin, Gregor, and Maggie. "We need to move quickly."

TWO HOURS LATER, WILL KNELT behind a bunch of rocks near the point. Plenty of tree cover and a rough firth would keep them from being discovered. The four grouped together and planned. "How many do you see?" Will asked. "I see three."

"Aye, as do I. Baines is closest to the river." Maggie whispered. "I'm going after him. If I have to kill the bastard, I will."

Will grasped her hand. "If you cannot control your temper, then I'll go after him. You cannot kill him, or you'll be hung. Whether he's involved in something illegal or not, he's still nobility. Promise me you'll maim and not kill."

"All right, but I'll do what I must." The man was a blight in England and needed to be put out of commission.

"Another just joined them," Gregor said. "I'll bet the one standing next to Baines is his marshal," he said, pointing. "He's a beast. Will, Gavin, and I can take the other two out while you and Maggie head for Baines and the marshal. I don't see any others. Where the hell is he keeping the lasses?"

Maggie said, "He's probably selling other cargo. Molly and Tormod search out stolen merchandise for the Crown all the time—metals, wool, whisky, all headed overseas. We have to find his stash, but there are so many rocks and brush in the area, it could be anywhere. We'll have to keep him alive to find out."

Will held his hand out to both of them. "Quiet. I think I hear something."

Gavin said, "You do. 'Tis a ship, though 'tis still a distance out."

"Then we move now. Are you ready, Maggie? I'm running behind you. You take first move for surprise. You go for Baines and I'll grab his friend."

Maggie nodded and then burst into a dead run, not waiting for another signal. Will motioned to the other two and ran behind her. Once again, he admired her running—she was quick, quiet, and sleek—like an animal tracking its prey. He had no doubt she could handle herself, and sure enough, she grabbed Baines from behind, tripped his legs out from under him and tackled him to the ground. The very next moment, she turned him face up and placed her dagger at his throat. Damn, but she was smooth, too. Didn't matter that she weighed probably half her opponent's weight.

Will grabbed the marshal, holding him against his chest, his knife at his throat.

The two struggled a bit, but once Will's dagger drew blood, the man stilled. Gavin and Gregor made their way over, their bows pulled with arrows now aimed at Baines and the marshal. "We took care of the other two, put them to sleep for a while."

Maggie said, "Where are the lasses, Baines?" She had her knee in the center of his belly, her full weight on him.

Baines smirked. "You think you can hold me down for long? Who the hell are you? Do you know who I am? I'll throw you in gaol for daring to touch me. You'll never be able to contain me and my men."

Maggie's left hand held her dagger. "Is that so?" Without looking away from Baines, she said over her shoulder, "Shoot him if he moves, Gavin."

She returned her attention to Baines and said, "Let me see if I can help your memory along." Then she pushed away from the earl, pulled her right arm back and hit him square in the bollocks with her fist. "Death is what you deserve, you bastard, but I'm not allowed to kill you. Still, seems only right I make you pay for some of your past deeds."

Baines choked and spat, writhing into a ball of pain.

She brought her face close to his. "My mother is Gwyneth Ramsay. Do you remember her? And that was for touching my sister when she was young. And for the beatings, though I think that deserves a hit to the other one."

She promptly kneed him, making sure her aim was true.

Will whistled. "Lass, let up or you'll lose him." The pain of two such shots would be enough to make most men faint dead away.

The marshal, still in Will's grasp, pulled one leg up for protection and whispered, "Geezus."

She spun around toward him and said, "He deserves it for all he's done to me, my sister, and countless other lasses."

Then she pivoted back to Baines. "And must I remind you that you left a lass to die back in your castle? You've got another one coming for that."

"Hit him again and you will lose him," Will repeated. "His eyes are rolling back."

She lowered her dagger and pulled the earl up by grabbing his leine, slapping his cheek. "Don't you dare pass out on me. Do you hear me, you piece of shite? You're such a tough man when you're hitting a wee lass, are you not? Where is that tough man now?"

He shook his head at her, so she pulled her knee back as if to deliver another blow between his legs. His eyes bugging out in alarm, he pointed wordlessly to a group of trees.

She let go of him and said, "Gavin, he's yours. Kill him if you need to. I'll see if he's telling the truth or not."

Maggie ran over to the trees, and after Gregor confirmed he'd keep watch on the marshal, Will followed directly behind her. He heaved out a sigh of relief when he saw a lone woman standing before several crates of loot.

"Who the hell are you?" the woman asked.

"I'm the lass who's about to give you a headache." Maggie pulled her fist back and punched her full on in the face, causing her head to snap back before she crumpled to the ground. Numerous crates sat in the area, so she pointed for Will to cover one section while she took care of the other.

Off to the side, he saw a plaid on the ground, two tiny forms huddled beneath it. "Over here." He knelt beside them and placed his hand on one child's neck while Maggie did the same with the other. "I think they're alive."

Maggie teared up. "Aye. This must be Emma, she's a wee bit smaller. Mayhap she gave them a sleeping potion. Will," she said, swiping at her tears, "Look how they clung to each other trying to stay warm. Their skin is so pale." Emma's hair was a pale blonde while Geva's was more golden, tiny curls at the end.

Will rubbed her arm and kissed her cheek. He loved that Maggie had such a soft heart, but he had to keep her moving. "Remember where we are. We need to get them to a safe place. Now, pick her up and let's get the hell out of here."

They scooped up the lassies and found their way back to Gavin and Gregor. "Take their weapons and throw them into the firth," Will said. "Then they won't follow us. The ship will be here shortly, so we'll leave them the rest of their cargo. Let's go."

They raced back to their horses, but Will heard Baines's last comment. "You'll pay for this, Ramsays. This is not over."

Maggie shouted back. "You're right, 'tis not. We'll be back." She turned for a moment to face her one-time tormentor. "I still owe you, you bastard, and I pay back my debts."

CHAPTER FOURTEEN

M AGGIE LET TEARS RUN DOWN her cheeks all the way back. Where were her parents? She'd thought they would meet up with them along the way, but they'd not seen any sign of them. How she prayed they were both safe.

She constantly checked the golden-haired lass in front of her. The bairn was still completely unconscious. Perhaps it was best that she'd been drugged. She wasn't as cold as Beatris had been, and she didn't look as though she'd been starved. The other lass rode with Will.

They set a grueling pace, but Maggie would not stop or even slow it. Her mind churned with all they had discovered.

How many more lassies like Beatris, Geva, and Emma were out there? How many more orphans, children kidnapped from their homes or taken into service under false pretenses were sold for slavery or even worse, for twisted sexual desires? Her own mother had been loaded onto a ship by evil men intent on selling her as a slave. Seeing such depravity with her own eyes had changed her.

Though she'd sought out Randall Baines in the hopes of giving Molly closure, that one decision had completely changed her life and given her a new purpose. Could she convince her parents to support her in this search for the victims of the depraved? Was there a chance Will would want to embark on this journey with her?

Gavin drew his horse up next to her. "Will she live, Maggie?"

"Aye, I think so."

Will drew up on the other side of her as soon as they reached a wider portion of the road. "Nice job back there, lass."

She smiled at him. "My thanks."

Gregor's voice echoed behind her, "Your mother will be proud."

"Though my bollocks are aching a wee bit from the sight of it," Gavin said. "He deserved it, of course, but warn me next time so I can close my eyes first. 'Twas painful to watch."

To their surprise, they were greeted by two figures on horseback once they drew close to Will's grandsire's land. Maggie let out a sigh of relief when she realized it was her mother and father. "More lassies?" her mama asked, her eyes going wide at the sight of them.

Maggie pulled on the reins of her horse. "Aye, Mama. Two more. Geva and Emma were with Beatris."

"Where did you find them?" Logan asked. "We've been all over Edinburgh searching for Baines, but no one we spoke to knew aught about him. It was as if he didn't exist in Edinburgh."

"Near the firth," Will replied. "A large ship was coming close to shore, and there were many crates stacked up, probably bound for the east. These were the only two girls we found."

"Maggie, you didn't kill anyone, did you?"

"Nay, only maimed, Papa."

They made it back to the small cottage, where two Ramsay guards were roasting meat outside for everyone. The others were gathered about.

Simone stood waiting in the doorway, and her face brightened the moment she saw the lasses. "You found them?"

"Aye, we did, but they're asleep," Maggie said. "I think they've been given a potion. Tell Beatris not to worry."

Simone clapped her hands and ran back inside, probably to tell Beatris the happy news. A moment later, as the group was dismounting, she carried her sister back outside balanced on her hip.

Once they'd settled the sleeping bairns inside, they left the cottage to make plans away from the wee ears. Will's hand settled on Maggie's lower back as they moved out. One glance at him calmed her, something she savored but did not quite understand.

This was not over as far as she was concerned. They'd take the lassies back to Ramsay land and help them heal, but her vendetta against Randall Baines was now stronger than ever. She briefly filled her parents in on the situation. "What do we do now, Papa?" she asked as she tied her horse to a nearby tree.

"All that you've told me is concerning, but your mother and I cannot go after Baines just yet. We have a more important issue we must deal with first. And I ask you to await our return before going off on your own again, Maggie."

"More important than three lassies being kidnapped? Papa, in another hour those two wee ones would have been gone forever, sent to their fates on some massive vessel. What could be more horrid?" Nothing could be more imperative than stopping Baines.

"You and Will must stay here," he insisted stubbornly. "Your mother and I will return home."

That thought didn't upset her, but she couldn't help but wonder why her sire would make such a demand, especially since he barely knew Will. He usually had a good reason for everything he did. "Why, Papa?"

"Because we found out that Baines has sent a sheriff of Edinburgh to arrest Molly for attacking his guards. I spoke with the sheriff and he normally would not act on such a false claim, but since Baines is a titled Englishman, he must take action. He conferred with King Alexander first, who promised to send a missive to the English king with his concerns. Even so, he will have to bring her in for questioning. I tried to convince him to wait, but Baines is being boorish. The king said he had to act, though Baines will not be allowed onto Ramsay land. We must get back to keep watch on your sister."

The merest of whispers escaped her lips. "Nay, not Molly." It was unbearable to think of Molly locked in her cell for something *she* had done…all because she'd wanted to help her sister. "Papa, you must stop them. The king won't allow it, will he? 'Tis not true. I'm the one who's at fault. She'll never be able to withstand riding a horse in her condition. Please, I should go with you."

"Nay, because if he sees you, he'll arrest you, also. I can only handle having one of my daughters being arrested. You'll not do that to me. We will keep you posted. If we get there first, naught will happen."

"Will and I were both there. Neither of us wounded to kill. Baines is lying to the king, I tell you." Will moved directly behind her, and she leaned back against him, grateful for his support and not caring what her sire thought.

"Aye, I believe you, but the man can issue his own punishment for any perceived crimes against his earldom. The sheriff will have to get past me if he tries to take Baines's grievances out on your sister."

Her sire began to pace, his hands on his hips, but he stopped, spinning around to face all of them. "Gwynie, this cannot wait the night. We'll take the guards with us and leave Gavin and Gregor here with the lassies. They aren't well enough to travel yet. Will, I promise you we'll return for them."

Maggie couldn't stop herself. She launched herself at her sire, throwing her arms around him. "Stop them, Papa, please. Don't let them take Molly away. She's in a bad enough state as it is."

"I agree. 'Tis why we leave now. Promise me you'll stay

here, Maggie, and we'll go now. I can't worry about two of my daughters." The look her sire gave her was not to be denied.

Maggie pulled back and nodded her head, unable to speak for fear she'd collapse into a barrage of tears. Oh, what had she done…

"Gwynie, let's move." He helped her mount, then whistled for the Ramsay guards to join them.

Her father's parting words were simple. "MacLerie, keep her here."

M AGGIE DID HER BEST TO keep herself calm, but the only way she could do that was to keep busy. Fortunately, there was plenty to do. If not, she'd vomit over the fear that Molly would be arrested for a crime she hadn't committed.

Gavin and Gregor caught a couple of rabbits to add to the food supply while Will's grandsire made more soup. They ate well with meat aplenty.

Geva and Emma had awakened just before the meal, totally confused, but the sight of their friends, free and happy, quickly calmed them down. They were beyond relieved to hear that they'd been taken away from Baines and would not be returning.

"Will we all go together, my lady?" Geva had asked Maggie.

"Aye, we shall keep you together, and I promise you'll not have to endure any beatings." She tousled wee Emma's hair as the lassie clapped her hands together in excitement.

"We're very good with the needle, my lady," Emma whispered. "We'll sew linens and tunics. Whatever you need. Geva can finish a tunic by herself in a day."

Maggie leaned down to kiss her forehead. "We'll gladly use your skills, but never for an entire day. You'll also be a child and play with your friends."

Beatris glanced at the others and said, "But we're to make use of ourselves, are we not? We can work in the kitchens. Simone and I helped with baking."

The anxiety in her wee gaze made Maggie want to weep anew. "You'll not be working in our kitchens, Beatris," she said. "You are too young. All you must focus on now is getting better. You must eat. Simone and I will wash your clothing. You all need a bath tonight."

After supper, the men set up the tub for the lassies and then headed outside to give them some privacy. When Maggie finally had them settled down for the night an hour later, she blew the candles out and left the cottage in search of Will.

As soon as she saw him, she broke into a smile. Would the mere sight of him always affect her like that?

His grandsire moved toward the door. "You young'uns go on your way. I'll watch the wee ones."

Will laughed. "He'll be asleep before they are." He held his hand out to her. "Gavin and Gregor are out patrolling. Come and walk with me. The land is glorious here and the moon is full tonight."

She tucked her hand inside his and followed him down a well-worn path toward a burn, the sound of the rushing water a boon to her troubled soul. The refreshing smell of pine filled the air, soothing her, and she was quite pleased when Will pulled her closer. "Come. We need to talk. I have something I must explain to you."

He led her over to a large rock near the burn, one with room enough for both of them to comfortably sit. Once they were settled there, side by side, he laced his fingers between hers.

"Is something wrong, Will?" Though there hadn't been any time to think their relationship through, she had strong feelings for him, feelings she'd never expected to have for a man. What if he was about to push her away? To tell her they didn't suit?

"Nay—" he squeezed her hand, "—but I want to tell you why I've been in hiding. 'Tis time. I'll start by telling you that I've spent some of my time over the last two years living in a cave just up this ravine. 'Tis up high and well hidden, so 'tis safe for me, and it allows me to keep watch on my grandsire without putting him at risk. Whenever I'm not here, I'm traveling. 'Tis my only way to encounter others since…well, 'tis what I must explain to you."

What was he about to tell her? Anticipation tightened her muscles as she looked at him, waiting as patiently as she could for him to speak. She could tell this was difficult for him because of the tension in his jaw. He stared at his boots for a bit before he finally began.

"This is hard for me, but I don't wish to hide anything from you…and if this changes how you feel about me, then I would like to know now."

He cocooned her hand in both of his, fidgeting his boots back and forth on the rock, so she thought she'd help him along. "Will, it would have to be pretty bad for me to change how I feel about you already."

He smiled and said, "I'm glad you think so, but I won't hold you to it." He cleared his throat. "I never knew my sire. He walked out on my mother when I was two summers old. We lived quite a bit north of here, in a small cluster of cottages not far from Clan MacLaren. My mother loved to hike the hills and the mountains in search of wildflowers and plants she could use for healing. I usually went along to protect her and to hunt. We visited Grandpapa quite a bit to bring him meat because his eyes no longer see well enough for him to hit anything but a giant boar…and only then if it stands still for him. One day, we came upon a lad lying in a clearing with an arrow in his belly. He still breathed, though my mother didn't think he would live for long. My mother had the special healing gift. She used herbs, aye, but she could also heal with her hands. Grandpapa says 'twas the heat of her hands that could seal a person's wounds."

He paused to gather his thoughts before he spoke again, staring off into the trees. "My mother knew she could never allow anyone to witness her healing lest she be considered a witch. It was her greatest fear, probably because 'tis the reason my father left. He could not accept her gift. She set her hand across the lad's wound and he eventually opened his eyes. We didn't realize the others were there until the lad glanced over her shoulder."

Will squeezed her hand before he continued. "It was the most difficult day of my life. Four men came upon us. While one was grateful and thanked my mother for what she'd done, the other three became crazed and accused her of witchery. I could not hope to take them all on by myself, so I ran for help. She screamed at me to keep running, but I was intent on saving her. By the time I returned with my grandsire, they had her tied to a post and a fire was set to the brush at her feet."

"Oh, Will. I'm so sorry. That must have been horrible for you."

"I wanted to stay and watch, but she yelled at me to run, so my grandsire pulled me away. More and more men continued to arrive. There was naught we could do at that point, though I kicked my grandsire twice when he carried me off.

"But I'll never forget the three men who'd accused her, especially the one who started the fire at her feet. I swore vengeance against him one day."

She cupped his cheek and gave him a light kiss to let him know how much he meant to her. How much hearing the truth meant to her.

"My mother was the warmest and most giving person I've ever known, and I still miss her every day. I'll never forget the screams that carried to me as we ran from the woods, I often hear them in my sleep. I swore I would find her killer one day."

Maggie couldn't bring herself to ask him for the rest of the story. She knew in her heart what had happened. He'd sought vengeance just as she felt compelled to do. She gazed into his eyes, but couldn't stop her own from misting. She understood exactly how he felt.

"Aye, I know your thoughts and 'tis true. A year after her death, I followed him into the woods. I waited until he was alone and killed him with my own dagger. He was brother to the laird of the MacEwans. And the lad my mother saved was the laird's son. The king has asked for me to be brought to court, but I'll not let them take my life. 'Tis why I run. I fear someday I'll have a noose cast around my own neck."

"But you dealt that man justice."

"Did I?" He rubbed his thumb across the back of her hand. "You understand, but others say I took the law into my own hands."

"So that explains your reputation as a vigilante."

"The MacEwans believe me guilty of murder and want me to stand in judgment, but I refuse to go to court. They burned my mother alive. There is no excuse for that. Not in my eyes. They did not wait to bring her to court, so I did not either." He stood and moved over to the edge of the clearing, staring up at the sky.

"I only wish I could have saved her." He settled his hands on his hips and said, "Instead, I try to prove my worth by helping other people. When I am finally caught, I hope there will be people who can vouch for me. If it does not save my life, at least it will help others understand what kind of man I am."

"My clan will stand up for you. Justice is not wrong. You stood up for your mother as I will stand up for my sister and those poor lasses."

Turning to face her, he traced a finger down her cheek, sending a shiver through her. "My mother often told me that things happen for a reason, and you may not understand them for many moons. Mayhap I understand her meaning now. She was also always after me to find a lass to marry. She feared I'd live my life alone because there were no lasses my age near us. She feared she'd have to send me away someday."

She could swear there were tears in his beautiful eyes, something that made her want to get even closer to him.

"We must make your mother proud, you and I," she said.

"And how are we to do that when she'll never know what we do?" He sat on a rock and tugged her onto his lap, running his thumb over her lower lip.

"She'll know. Now we have even more purpose than we did before. 'Tis settled in my mind. We do this for my sister Molly *and* for your mother."

He leaned down and sucked on her lower lip a bit before he kissed her deeply. Before she was ready, he pulled away and pressed his forehead to hers, his eyes closed.

"What exactly are we doing? You make me forget my thoughts," he rasped.

She sighed deeply, then said, "You make my heart flutter whenever we're together, Will MacLerie, and I like it. Please don't stop. If we can settle all this chaos, then mayhap we'll have the opportunity to chase our hearts and our thoughts. But until then, we make Baines pay for hurting wee ones."

CHAPTER FIFTEEN

WILL TRUDGED BACK TOWARD THE cottage the next morn after taking care of his needs and filling two buckets with fresh water for the house full of wee ones. He couldn't help but smile at the thought of how much life had changed. A moon ago, he and his grandsire had both been alone, living in fear. Today, the house was full of chattering young ones, and Will, who had thought he'd spend what remained of his life alone, had met someone he trusted and could confide in. He was surprised at how much Grandpapa enjoyed the company, though he had set the lassies to doing some wee chores for him. He was always thinking, that man.

The door flew open and Maggie almost ran right into him. "Good. I was coming for you." She gave him a strange look that he didn't quite know how to interpret.

"Is something wrong? The lassies are better?"

"Aye, they are fine. Geva and Emma are both chatterboxes. Beatris is still weak, but her color is much improved today, and she's already announced she's hungry."

He held the buckets up for her. "I brought water. Grandpapa will get the porridge going."

"I'll help you bring them in," she said, "and then we need to talk." Something told him he was not going to like whatever she had to say, but there was no putting her off. She reached for one of the pails he held, but he indicated with his head that she should open the door for him instead. He squeezed past her and winked as he walked over to the hearth with the buckets.

"Just what we needed, lad," his grandsire said. "My thanks. I'll get that porridge going."

"Grandpapa, I'll be right back." The older man just waved at him, pleased to have something to do this morn, no doubt. He often complained of boredom and loneliness, and now he had a house full of laughter.

Will was about to step outside when Simone bustled up to his grandsire and asked, "Is there any needlework we could help you with? Geva and I are good seamstresses. We can repair any holes in your clothing."

He heard his grandfather chuckle with glee. "Lass, I have some sewing for you and I'll give you a double serving of porridge if you can fix my favorite breeches."

Laughing to himself, Will stepped into the brisk morning air and smiled at Maggie, who'd stayed outside. "You look lovely this morn, lass."

Maggie rolled her eyes, but then surprised him with a huge smile. His mother was right. She had advised him he could win a lass over with words more than aught else. He waited to see what Maggie had to say, giving her the chance to gather her thoughts as she chewed on her bottom lip, something he wished he were doing instead.

She glanced over her shoulder, then leaned toward him to whisper, "We must go."

He couldn't have been more shocked. "Your sire said to keep you here. You promised him you'd stay."

"That was yesterday. I thought we'd at least have seen a messenger by now. I cannot tolerate the waiting. I must know if those men have come for my sister."

"But Molly, we cannot take the lassies with us, and I really don't think it would be wise to leave four of them with Grandsire. He doesn't have enough food for all of them. We can hunt. He cannot."

She crossed her arms and paced a small circle, chewing on the inside of her cheek this time. "We can leave Gavin and Gregor behind. They'll hunt enough for twelve people."

"Aye, they will, but do you think they'll agree to stay? They're off hunting now." Will had serious doubts that the two lads would follow directions any more than Maggie seemed inclined to do. "Besides that, he could never protect them. We need to stay here to guarantee their safety. Have you forgotten my promise to your father?"

She rolled her eyes, reluctant to concede, but then squared her shoulders and stood tall. "You're right. Gavin and Gregor should know more about wee lasses after growing up with so many sisters, but they don't." Then she moved closer to him and tipped her head up, hoping to tease him for a kiss. "And while I don't mind pushing my father, I wouldn't advise you to ignore his wishes. I think I recall him saying something about castration."

His expression changed at the last word, his skin turning a bit green. She stepped back to stare at him. "You're the Wild Falconer. How can you be afraid of my father?"

"Your father? The beast of the Highlands? I don't know. Mayhap because we've all heard how he challenged your sister's husband with a sword? How the man jumped down a cliff to save her, and he *still* wasn't good enough for your sire? And before you ask, I'm fearful of your mother, too. Everyone in the Highlands has heard how she killed a man by pinning his bollocks to a tree and..."

She waved her hands in a gesture of defeat. "All right. I understand." When he put it like that, her parents *did* sound daunting. Cailean *had* gone through hell for her sister Sorcha. How had Molly managed to gain a husband with such little fuss?

Will swaggered over to her and set his finger under her chin, lifting her lips back toward him. "I'm more than thrilled with you, Maggie Ramsay, but I cannot deny that our courtship might have been easier had you been the daughter of another." He kissed her, ravaging her mouth with a need that took her by surprise. She reached up to wrap her hands around his neck, feeling the sudden need to touch him everywhere. He ended the kiss with a peck on her nose. "But then I doubt you'd have the passion roiling inside you. Your parents have taught you to stand up and fight for your beliefs, and that's one of the things I love most about you."

She did her best not to widen her eyes at the word he used, but she never had the chance to ask him more about his declaration.

The sound of horses' hooves cut their conversation short. Maggie grabbed her dagger, Will grabbed his bow, and they both moved away from the cottage toward the sound of the horses.

Five men, all wearing Ramsay plaids. Maggie sheathed her knife and shouted, "Cailean, what is it?"

The man in the lead replied, "I'm to take you to Edinburgh. Your sire's orders. Gavin and Gregor will travel with us. The guards will remain here until Aunt Brenna arrives with a contingency to take the lassies back to Ramsay land."

Just then, Gavin and Gregor emerged from the woods with two rabbits and a duck. "We heard you coming. We're leaving?" Gavin asked.

"Aye," the one called Cailean said. "You have five minutes. We're meeting your sire in Edinburgh."

"What's happened?" Maggie cried, kneading her hands until they were white.

"Naught yet. Just following orders. Your sire barked orders so fast no one questioned him. Grab your things. Is this lad coming with us, then?"

Maggie spun around to stare at him. "Please, Will?" she asked, her eyes begging him. He knew exactly what she was thinking.

She believed the worst. Her sister was in deep trouble. Mayhap she'd even been brought to the king as a prisoner.

He'd go along to support her no matter what.

"Come with us?"

He knew he risked running into someone who recognized him, but he was willing to take the chance for her. "Aye. I'll talk to Grandpapa and be right back." He glanced at Cailean and said, "I'm Will MacLerie. Looks like I'll be traveling with you."

Cailean nodded and said, "MacAdam. I welcome anyone who can use a bow. I don't expect to find many friends along the way."

———————

T HE CLOSER THEY CAME TO Edinburgh, the more Maggie's hands trembled. She'd begged Cailean to tell her more, but he insisted he didn't have anything else to tell her. He'd been out on patrol right up until he received his orders.

"I may have married your sister, but I'm not foolish enough to question your sire unless I've no choice. He'd still love face-to-face combat with me any time." Cailean shook his head. "Hmmph. Not a fool. I was once, and I learned. Never again."

"But you beat him, Cailean. That's what Sorcha says," she replied.

"Because he gave in. We're going to the royal castle, though, and I expect he'll already be there. We're to wait if he's not."

Once in Edinburgh, Cailean led their party through the busy streets.

Gavin came up beside her and whispered, "Something's going on. Too many people are headed toward the castle."

She glanced at Will, who was doing his best to stay in the middle of the group so as not to be noticed. She held back to speak to him. "If you're worried about being discovered then stay back. We can meet up later."

"Nay, I'm staying with you. Besides, no one is paying me any mind. They're all focused on the castle. When we near the royal castle, I may have to hide, but I'll only do it if 'tis necessary. Expect me to stay nearby at all times." He acted confident about this decision, not trying to hide from anyone's view. "Besides, they may have a warrant out for my arrest, but the king has never seen me, and the MacEwans haven't seen me in two years. While I'm no taller, I have built up my strength and the breadth of my shoulders. I dress differently so 'tis a possibility that no one would recognize me, even our king."

As soon as they drew near the castle, she could hear her father's bellows above the sounds of the gathering. Nerves prickled at her. That could not be good… Cailean motioned for them to leave their horses tied near the town stables, then grabbed Maggie's hand and pulled her behind him. "You must stay with me. Do not think of leaving me."

Will was behind her, his hand on the small of her back, pulsing warmth and comfort through her, and as they began to move through the crowd, he fell in on her other side. He and Cailean cleared the way for them, Gavin and Gregor behind them. They finally made their way up to the gates, and she screamed at the horrifying sight before her. "Molly!"

Her legs buckled but Will caught her, setting her in front of him. Cailean stood to the side, attempting to get her sire's attention, but Will caught his waving arm. "Wait," he said. "See what is going on first. For all we know, they could be looking for Maggie, too."

While Cailean shot her a surprised look, he didn't hesitate to step in front of her. Will did the same, and the human shield of two extremely large men blocked almost everyone's view of her. She managed to find a way to peek around Cailean's arm to assess the situation.

Molly was on a platform in the center of the castle courtyard, tied to a post with her arms shackled to a metal bar over her head. She held her chin high, but Maggie could tell she was in pain.

King Alexander III stood in front of the platform, Randall Baines on one side, her sire, Tormod, and Uncle Micheil on the other side. Micheil's son David stood behind him.

The king said, "Tell me your story again, Baines? It better be good because you're accusing one of my most loyal subjects from one of my foremost clans. In fact, take the shackles from her arms. She's not going anywhere."

A guard did as the king instructed while Baines launched into his rant. "She killed two of my warriors and one housekeeper," he bellowed. "I want her hung. 'Tis only fair. You need to make an example of her. Too much random killing is being done by the savage Scots."

The king quirked his brow. "The savage Scots, you say? Are you daring to call my people savage?"

"Yes." Baines glared from one person to the other in the crowd, strutting about as he used to do in Wingate, using his body language and tone of voice to intimidate people. While she didn't know the king well, she knew Baines's tactics would never work on her sire or Uncle Micheil. He was wasting his breath, though she guessed he was putting the show on for the people outside the gates as much as the ones inside.

Her father shot back, "Since she has two broken ribs and hasn't been off our land in over a fortnight, I fail to see how you can accuse her. And where did this take place? Here or in England?"

"In England. At my castle at Wingate. I wasn't there…"

"Then how the hell can you be so sure it was her? Impossible. She was nowhere near England." Logan turned to their king. "My king, I swear she has been bedbound by her ribs for days. She was in training when she took the fall in a ravine on our land. I will vouch for her."

"I'm inclined to believe Logan Ramsay," the king announced, crossing his arms in front of him.

"He's a liar," Baines declared loud enough for all to hear. Out of the back of the castle came another man—

Baines's marshal. He strode up to the platform, took one look at Molly, and said, "King, I saw her do it. She's guilty."

Maggie thought she would heave off to the side. She grabbed Will's hand in a death grip, glancing at him briefly until she brought her gaze up to meet her sister's. Molly had finally noticed her and locked gazes with her. Her sister was shaking her head almost imperceptibly.

She knew exactly what it meant—to keep quiet. She knew it was Maggie whom Baines should be accusing, but she was telling her to be quiet.

The king could hang Molly for murder.

Baines could bring her back to his castle for disciplining. He could lock her in gaol.

He could insist she be taken to the English king.

Courts didn't often hang women. Molly could be imprisoned for the rest of her life.

She could be whipped until she was nearly dead.

Just like so many times before.

Maggie couldn't allow it. Never again would she let her sister be punished for a crime she'd committed.

The king said, "I have other issues to attend to. I'll lock her in a cellar chamber and make a decision later. I need time to research this matter. You," he pointed to Baines, "will stay away from her. I'll speak to you on the morrow."

Maggie glanced at Will and whispered, "I'm sorry." His face tightened up with alarm.

The king said, "Lock her up!" The group was split in their responses, some hailing insults at the English earl and others cheering for him. Her sire bellowed with a fury she'd never seen before. The king moved over to whisper to her father while the crowd carried on.

She could take no more of it.

Maggie shook the metal bars that kept them outside the courtyard and screamed, "She didn't do it! I did. Lock me up, not her."

Her father and uncle whirled around, shocked to hear

her confession. Her sire was shaking his head no, as was her sister. Though she couldn't read her sire's expression, he'd always taught her honesty was the best. It was time for her to be honest and save her sister.

"I did it. I'm guilty." She screamed her confession so all would hear her. "I fired an arrow at the woman because she was beating a lass of ten summers. But he's still lying. I hit her in the shoulder, and she still lives, I'm sure of it. I hit another guard with an arrow and a third in the leg with a knife, but none of them were fatal injuries." Her hands gripped the iron of the gate with white knuckles. Cailean and Will now stood on either side of her, and Will had wrapped an arm about her waist, still protecting her. Still attesting to his love.

"I pray they've not heard of the reivers who chased us," he whispered.

Cailean gave him a surprised look. "The king does not care about reivers. They're thieves."

The earl pointed his finger at her. "That's the one. I was mistaken. Arrest her and lock her up. Hang her now. Whip her first. She's nothing but trouble. I want her held accountable for all the trouble she caused on English soil. My king will be hearing all about this, I promise you."

The mob went wild, jumping up and down, shaking their fists while the king conferred with his guards and her sire and uncle. Some called for her punishment, but more called for Baines to be sent back to England.

"Open the gates," King Alexander finally shouted.

A line of guards moved over to the entrance, lining up in preparation to keep the crowd from entering. Maggie stood glued to her spot, her self-appointed guards still beside her. Will leaned close to her ear and whispered, "I'll get you out, Maggie. Have faith in me."

"We'll go with him," Gavin said from behind her. Clearly he'd been close enough to hear. "This is not over. He's a bastard and a liar."

The moment the gates were opened, the king had the guards free Molly. Then he pointed at Maggie, who pushed away from them and ran to her sister, hugging her lightly so as not to hurt her. Her sire paced toward her like a wild animal. "What the hell have you done?" he asked in a low growl pitched only for their ears.

"I couldn't let her take my punishment again, Papa. 'Tis all because of what I did."

"But she works for the king. He would never hurt her. He was doing this for show."

"He said he would lock her up in the cellar."

"That was only to make the crowd happy. True, many support us because we're Scots, but some are simply out for blood. He told me he'd put her in the nicest chamber abovestairs and have his healer tend her. Now you've admitted to the crime Baines accused her of."

Uncle Micheil said, "Not to worry. We'll get her released. Diana's on her way and she'll bend the king's ear for a while. And while she's arguing with Alexander, David and I will get her out."

The guards pulled Maggie away from Molly and tied her hands behind her back. How had it come to this? She'd managed to save four wee ones and protect her sister, but now she was to be imprisoned. Things had gone from bad to worse. At least her sister was free—Molly needed time to heal—and with any luck, her family would be able to assist her.

Just before they took her inside, King Alexander came over to her and whispered, "You shouldn't have done that, lass. I have no choice now." He glanced over at the crowd and proclaimed, "Lock her in the cellar!"

She dropped her voice for only the king to hear. "But my king, has no one told you that we saved three lassies from being sold by that bastard? He was to sell them at the firth. Five, six, and seven summers. You cannot excuse that."

King Alexander's eyes bore into hers. "I have heard this tale. I will look into it, but for the moment my men must bring you inside. This crowd needs to be dispersed, and 'tis the only way. Trust me when I say that you will be treated with respect."

"Many thanks, my king." She bowed her head.

"Unfortunately, these things take time. I cannot make any promises as to how quickly this will be resolved. But I will keep him here while this issue is being sorted out. He'll not be allowed to go after more Scottish lassies, I promise you."

The guards' hands were all over her and she cringed from their touch as they led her inside the castle. Voices carried to her over the din of the crowd. King Alexander said, "Ramsays. Both of you in my solar. Baines, go to your own estate. I'll handle the situation from here."

One voice rang out over all the others—Will's.

"I'm coming for you. I'll never leave you."

She believed him. She had to.

CHAPTER SIXTEEN

———◆———

WILL WAS FRANTIC, BUT DIDN'T know where to go or what to do. Maggie's sire came over to them as soon as the group began to disperse.

"We'll get her out," Logan said. "Cailean, come with me to meet with the king. The rest of you stay the hell away from Baines and wait for me. There's an inn down the street." He pointed and tossed them a few coins before spinning on his heel and heading into the royal castle.

Gavin, who'd caught the coins, said, "I'm hungry. Papa gets his own chamber there. They know me. We can make our plans there without being overheard." The three of them—Will, Gavin, and Gregor—headed down the street together, but a voice stopped them in their tracks. "Wait for me. I'll join you."

Will turned around to see a dark-haired man dressed in a Drummond plaid heading toward them. He'd stood behind the gates with Logan and that other man.

"Another cousin," Gregor explained. "This is David, heir to the Drummond chieftain. His sire is inside with Uncle Logan."

Will introduced himself, and then the newly expanded group headed down the street toward the inn. He had to do something. He'd wait until it was dark, then he'd find his way into the castle.

Nothing would stop him. Not even Logan Ramsay himself.

He paced restlessly while Gavin spoke to the innkeeper. A moment later, the man nodded and said, "Of course, my lord. Follow me."

My lord? If Will had been eating anything, he would have choked. Gavin gave them a smug smile and followed the man to a private chamber with a table for six next to a large hearth. The sideboard was already filled with bread and ale.

"I shall have the serving maid bring your meat pies," the man said. At Gavin's nod, he left the room.

Will couldn't help himself. "My lord? Truly?"

"My sire is Logan Ramsay. I know my way around Edinburgh." If Gavin's chest popped out any farther, he wouldn't be able to eat.

Gregor said, "My sire was the old chieftain, and my brother is the present one. If anyone in this room is of noble blood, 'tis me." He glanced at the others, finally noticing David, who was watching the exchange with a quirked brow and crossed arms. "Well, besides you, David. We all know you're the heir to the lairdship."

David laughed and pulled out a chair. "No matter. I'm hungry. Sit and we'll come up with a plan."

No longer able to hold back, Will announced, "I'm not sure what the rest of you intend, but I'm going after Maggie as soon as 'tis dark." He grabbed a hunk of bread and deposited the rest of the loaf in the middle of the table for the others. Then he filled a couple goblets with ale and set them on the table. "Eat hearty because I'll not leave Edinburgh without her."

With that, he took a seat, looking from Ramsay to Ramsay to Drummond.

David held his hands up. "I'll gladly help, but what exactly transpired? Who's guilty? Maggie or Molly?"

Gavin and Gregor both replied, "Maggie."

Will glared at the two of them before turning back to look at David. "Baines is the only guilty party. Maggie and I came upon a woman beating a lass of ten summers in the middle of a crowd at Wingate. She fired an arrow into the woman's shoulder to force her to drop the whip. Two men came at Maggie. She injured them both to keep them from attacking. What Maggie said earlier was true. None were fatal injuries. The only explanation is Baines is lying because we stole his cargo."

"Cargo? What cargo?" David asked.

"Three lasses he was about to put on a ship headed for the east probably. We left plenty of crates full of goods to sell, but he wasn't happy about us taking the lasses. That's four lassies we took from him, counting the one beneath the whip. In fact, his parting words were something about vengeance."

"He's a bastard," Gregor said with a scowl. "I remember Aunt Gwyneth's stories about him from years ago."

"Then why is he still here?" Will asked. "Why hasn't anyone taken care of him before now? He's as crooked and slimy as they come."

"I've heard this tale many times over," David said, "so please allow me the pleasure to retell it, only I'll leave out the part about Auntie trussing his bollocks in front of the king. Aunt Gwyneth and Uncle Logan basically put an end to Baines's intention to marry a wealthy Scot. They revealed his mistreatment of Molly and Maggie to the king and also foiled his plan to kidnap my mother to take home as his mistress. He had no idea she was to be a laird. King Alexander sent him back to England as soon as his cruelty and lies were discovered. Hellfire, I wish I could have seen your parents in action when they were young, Gavin. My sire said they were unbelievable."

"That's a great tale," Will said, "but if King Alexander is aware of their differences, why would he believe Baines this time?"

Gavin and Gregor exchanged a look and shrugged their shoulders.

"Because he's the Earl of Wingate," David finally said. "He was only the son of the earl before. Now the king must at least pretend to listen to him. But knowing the background, he should know better. I'm sure Uncle Logan will remind our king of Baines's past."

"Why is the crowd supporting Baines? He's English, Maggie's Scottish. I thought they'd support her," Will asked.

David snorted. "I've seen this happen over and over. Much of the crowd doesn't care who is punished. They just hope blood will be spilled. There are many who support Maggie's cause, but they aren't nearly as vocal. The king knows his people are looking for a bit of drama, so he gives them what they want, yelling his demands. Inside, he'll probably wrap his arm around her shoulder. Is Aunt Gwyneth here? I didn't see her."

"She stayed home because Brigid and Jennet were so upset when they took Molly," Gregor said. "'Tis what the guards told me, anyway. We stayed at Will's grandsire's house last night with the rescued lasses."

Gavin added, "And I heard she told my father she was staying behind so she wouldn't kill Randall Baines with her bare hands, then cut his bollocks off and feed them to the wolves."

David spat his ale out and Gregor guffawed. Will could not help but smile. "So that's where Maggie gets it from."

"What do you mean?" David asked.

"When we caught Baines on the shore of the firth, Maggie tackled him as hard as any man I've ever seen and then punched and kneed him in his bollocks—twice—to get him to tell us where the two lassies were hidden."

"Ouch," David said, instinctively covering his private area.

"I think she said the first one was for touching her sister. Is that right, Gavin?"

Gavin grew serious, something that didn't seem to happen often. "Aye. Baines did some nasty things to Molly. His mother liked to beat them."

Will hated to imagine wee Maggie in such a position.

How had the two sisters survived such treatment? But he knew—because of their strong spirits and Logan and Gwyneth Ramsay.

Silence fell as Gavin's words settled in their minds.

Will said, "I stand my ground. I'm going after her as soon as 'tis dark. Who's interested in going with me?"

"What about my sire?" Gavin asked. "I think you should let him know your plans."

Will considered this advice for a moment. "Think you he will support me?"

Gavin nodded. "He'll want her out, and it would be better if it wasn't him sneaking down into the cellar. He'll try to be proper in the royal castle."

"I agree," David said. "He'll be glad to hear you offer."

"Then I'll talk to him first. Who wishes to go along?"

Three hands shot into the air.

———◆———

MAGGIE STRUGGLED WITH HER CAPTORS as they shoved her along a passageway and then down the stairs into the dark caverns in the cellars of the castle. Four men held her even though her hands were tied behind her back. No one said a word to her until they reached the bottom of the staircase.

The guard to the right of her in front reached back and rubbed her bottom. "I'm glad 'tis you and not your sister. Your arse is much nicer." He gave her a twisted grin and waggled his brow at her. "I cannot wait to see the rest of you."

"Take your disgusting hands away from me," she said.

The one on the left shook his head. "If you touch her, you're a fool. Have you forgotten who her sire is? I don't care what Baines says. He's an English fool, and she'll be out by the morrow. I'd keep your hands to yourself, or her father will skin you and hang you outside the gates for all to see."

The one in the back cursed. "And if her mother arrives, she'll do worse."

The bastard chuckled. "You two don't have any bollocks. If she's here until the morrow, that's one day I have to play with her. 'Tis nice to have a female prisoner for a change, and they're easy to intimidate."

The guard in the back spoke up again. "Apparently, he hasn't heard about Gwyneth Ramsay and what she does to men." The three who did know her mother's reputations exchanged grins as they looked at the touchy bastard.

"I'm not afraid of no woman."

One of the others snorted. "You should be if you value your bollocks."

"Aye?" the bastard asked. "This is how afraid I am of her mother and sire." He reached around to rub her bottom again, and Maggie spat in his eye.

She couldn't stop herself even though she knew he would swing at her. In fact, because she expected it, she did her best to bite him when he swung out. She must have caught his skin because he cursed and swung again, catching the side of her face with a loud crack. "The bitch bit me!"

Out of nowhere came a blur. Her sire grabbed the brute and the two flew through the air, landing in a heap ahead of them.

Her father had the scum by the throat. "You touch my daughter again and I'll flay you alive and feed you to the vultures, but only after I allow my wife to do as she wishes with your bollocks."

Maggie could see he had enough pressure on the guard's windpipe to cause the man's eyes to protrude a bit, though she guessed that was also a result of the man's belated fear.

Her father told the others, "Move along and lock her up so no one else can touch her. Any man who does will answer to me." He held the guard up and punched him directly in the face, the impact making a resounding crunch that echoed down the passageway. Then he tossed him back toward the stairs. "Get the hell out of here, you piece of shite."

King Alexander's voice echoed down to them at about the same time the guard landed at the bottom of the stairs. "What goes, Ramsay?"

"One of your guards dared to touch my daughter, my king."

Maggie was pushed inside the cell. One of the guards untied her hands, and the same man grabbed a stool from the passageway and set it inside the cell for her. Then the door slammed and the guard locked it with the key, but she noticed none of the guards dared to move any closer to her sire, their eyes staring at the activity in the stairwell.

The king hollered at the injured guard, "Get your lazy arse out of my castle. You'll report to the marshal."

The man rolled over, grumbling and moaning.

"Now, Erwin," the king said, "or I'll let Ramsay do whatever he wishes with you."

The bastard finally pushed himself to a standing position and must have headed up the stairs because everything suddenly quieted. The remaining guards silently stood sentry and her sire's face appeared between the metal slats of the cell. "Sit on the stool and I will take care of everything. I'll see that fresh water and bread are brought to you. Don't speak to anyone. You're safer here for now."

"Where's Molly?"

"Aunt Diana arrived. She's with her above stairs and has sent for a healer. They're not allowed down here. Once I've explained everything to the king, you'll be free, but Molly had a rough trip here with her restraints. I don't want her moved."

She could see how her sire struggled to control himself, this man who had done so much for her, beginning on the long-ago day he'd rescued the two of them from Baines's clutches. Though adopted, she and Molly had always been treated exactly the same as any of their siblings. "Papa, I'm sorry. I love you dearly for all you've done for my sister and me." She swiped at the tears sliding down her cheeks.

His fury calmed and she was glad of it. "I'll take care of everything. You have done naught wrong, but the king must justify his actions to the people and the King of England, especially when a member of English nobility is involved. We will expose Baines for the scoundrel he is. Until then, you must be patient and keep safe."

He spun on his heel and headed back down the passageway.

Maggie stared at her surroundings, wondering how it had come to this.

The stone cell was quite cold, and she gave a quick prayer of thanks for a mother who believed women had the intelligence to choose what they wore. Her leggings and tunic were warm and she had wool stockings on underneath to battle against the cold of the night. Her boots were of the best workmanship possible, sewn with her own careful stitches.

This had all started because her parents had chosen to give her and her sister away. Molly wasn't the only one who'd been chosen for a hateful reason, and she found herself dwelling on what she'd overheard all those years ago.

She'd been unable to sleep that night, and her parents' bickering voices had carried up through the rafters to their small sleeping loft.

"I see the way you look at her," her mama had said. "She's too attractive."

Her father had retorted, "Aye, I like looking at her. She's a beautiful child."

"Well, I'll not have her here causing trouble. I know what your thoughts are. I'm sending her with Molly."

"No!" Her father's objection had been louder than expected, but she'd often felt like she was his favorite because he would always call her over to sit on his lap.

"Yes. You chose Molly and gave me no say. I choose Maggie and give you no say. It's done. I'll take them both to the Baines castle in two days."

That conversation had replayed in her mind so many times that she'd lost count. She'd never told Molly because she was too embarrassed. Her own mother had disliked her and given her away. She remembered the venom her mother had spewed at her sire, how hateful her voice had sounded, and all because of her.

That was what beauty did for a lass.

She got off her stool and paced, looking at her new home. What would be her punishment? Was she to be hung? Beaten? Left here to rot? Spider webs hung from the ceiling, and there was a small pot in the corner that she'd rather not look at, let alone use. In the other corner was a pallet and a blanket. How long could one survive here without losing one's mind?

What kind of world punished those who fought for the helpless? She'd injured a woman who'd taken pleasure from beating bairns. Protected Emma and Geva from Baines and his guards.

Her sire would tell the king all they'd observed—the kidnapped lasses, the attempted sale—all of it. But would it be enough to free her?

She thought of Will, wondered if he would truly try and come for her. As soon as his smile entered her mind, she smiled with him. She'd never thought herself soft of heart, but somehow Will MacLerie had managed to change her mind. Though he was tall and strong, dark and handsome, it was his own kind heart and fierce bravery that had won her over.

A loud sound filtered in from outside, probably from the front of the castle. Her sire had often told them that the people of Edinburgh loved to march on the castle as a mob. They could be bloodthirsty, he'd said, always hoping for death or punishment. While she listened, they began to chant, their voices ringing out into the night. It had to be dark by now, so she imagined them carrying torches, their fists raised in the air. Her sire had said the worst deeds took place at night because the perpetrators hid in the shadows.

How she hoped they'd come here to condemn Randall Baines.

The more she listened, the more they chanted, but she couldn't make out their meaning. The space she sat in seemed to shrink and she jumped up, wishing she could push the walls out to widen the tiny space.

How she prayed Will was on his way.

CHAPTER SEVENTEEN

———————

WILL COULD BARELY CONTAIN HIS need to go after Maggie, but he knew the best man to help them had not yet arrived. When he finally heard the man's gruff voice outside the inn, he stopped pacing the private dining room, which he'd been doing since he finished eating, and sat with the others to wait for him.

Logan Ramsay burst into the room, his brother Micheil beside him. He motioned to the innkeeper for more ale and meat pies and then closed the door behind them.

"Papa. What have you learned?" Gavin asked.

"The situation is not good at the moment, but justice will prevail, or I'll be on a killing rampage in two days." He sat in a chair and motioned for Micheil to take the other empty chair at the table.

"Where's Cailean?" Gregor asked.

"I sent him back to Will's grandsire with a few other guards. If Brenna hasn't brought the lassies back to Ramsay land and they're well enough to travel, I wish to bring them here to prove Baines is lying."

"Events are not unfolding as we'd hoped," Micheil said. "Diana's furious and letting her ire be heard everywhere, but our king isn't listening and Baines won't show his face. Apparently, the King of England sent a messenger saying he demands justice for Randall Baines."

"That one action by the English king is slowing our quest down," Logan said. "But I will not stop until Maggie is freed."

"Where are they both now?" Will asked.

"Molly is being seen by a healer with Diana at her side," Logan replied. "She'll be fine—she just needs to rest for a bit. I've sent a messenger to tell Gwynie that Molly has been set free, but I'll be keeping her here for a while."

"And Maggie?" Will persisted.

"Maggie is in a cell in the basement."

Will bolted out of his chair. "Is she chained like an animal, too?" His fury could not be stopped. Was her father truly planning to let her spend the night in a cell?

"Now calm down, William. I've made sure she's fed decent food, and she's unchained. They've placed a stool inside and there's a pallet with a blanket. There's a mob surrounding the castle right now, hoping for a hanging. They're begging for any bloodshed, so do not think it has aught to do with her. They're simply bored. 'Tis the only reason I've allowed her to stay there. Well, and one other..."

Will almost shouted at him, he was so furious. "What other reason could you possibly have to see your daughter held prisoner?"

Logan leapt out of his own chair and got close to his face. "I have my reasons, and I suggest you don't question them." Will was the taller of the two by far, but Maggie's sire was still an intimidating man. He was referred to as a beast by many. Still, Will did not back down. What kind of man wanted his daughter imprisoned?

"She's safer there," David said softly.

"Aye," Gregor added. "Maggie has been acting on emotion, not thinking clearly, and this way he knows where she is at all times."

Gavin added, "I fear she'd kill Baines for imprisoning Molly."

Logan whispered, "And *that* noose I would not be able to remove from her neck. I'm glad someone else has some sense. What no one else has mentioned is that she's one of the strongest warriors I have, both with her bow and her daggers. If she wants Randall Baines dead and she's in the same location, he'll be dead. This way, she cannot commit a crime."

Would the lads back out of their agreement to rescue her? Would they put their trust in a king who clearly cared more about politics than he did about the life of one lass?

"Why don't we all sit down and discuss this, come up with a plan?" Micheil said.

His calm tone only made Will more restless. He was ready to move. To carry out the promise he'd made her. He'd thought this through several times. Indeed, he'd thought of little else in the hours they'd been parted. "I'm going after Maggie, and I'm getting her out. No one here is going to stop me."

"Let's suppose you're fool enough to make the attempt and lucky enough to get her out," Logan said. "Then what will you do with her? If the mob gets ahold of the two of you, they'll hang you both. Until you can prove your innocence, traveling will be risky. Every reiver in the land will try to take you down for reward coins. There is no loyalty to Scotland when coins are involved."

Will could no longer sit still, but Logan was her sire so he decided to be respectful and stay calm, though every ounce of his being fought against him. "I will get her out. I've spent the past two years living in caves. I know where they all are, even the best-hidden ones. We'll travel from cave to cave, keep moving so they won't ever catch her. We'll stay hidden until this mess is cleared up."

Logan's voice came out in a hiss. "That's my daughter you're talking about cohabitating with."

"Then I'll find a priest and marry her first. I love your daughter, and I will not sit here while she's in the damp cellar of any castle. She is innocent. I have my ways." He turned to Gavin and Gregor, hoping they'd still be willing to help. "I ask you to follow me, so when I get her out, you can protect our backs until we get into the forests. Once we're there, I'll not need any help. She's as fast and sure-footed as anyone, but I do worry about the crowd. Will you help me?"

David stood up, glancing at his father, "Sorry, Papa, if you don't agree, but I'm going with him. Randall Baines is the man who tried to kidnap my mother...and it sounds like he has continued to hurt lasses."

Gregor stood up and said, "We'll follow, too."

"The hell you will," Logan shouted. "You'll stay away. You'll let us decide what's best."

Gavin shook his head. "Papa, have you not taught us to stand up for what is right, to defend the helpless, to do the honorable thing at all times? At the present, my sister is helpless. I'm going to help Will rescue her because she would do the same for me. I hope you'll go along with us. If naught else, you can draw a map of the castle so he knows exactly where to find her.

"I know the castle well," David said. "I can draw the map and Logan can provide details on her whereabouts." He left to find the innkeeper to find parchment and ink.

Micheil stood up, still a powerful man after so many years, much like his brother. He grasped his brother's shoulder and said, "Logan, I know you're emotionally involved, but I'm of the opinion to let the young ones take over. You must stay on the king's good side, and so must I. They needn't do the same. I doubt the king would even recognize any of them. They're in the right, and they aren't acting any differently than you and I did when we were their age."

To his surprise, Logan relented for a moment.

"What about your birds?" he asked. "You'll need a wee bit more protection than just the two of you once you're outside Edinburgh. I cannot send guards with you."

Will caught Logan's gaze, surprised to see a bit of respect in his eyes. "I'll have my falcons follow us. Sealgar, the peregrine, will attack if he senses any danger. Stoirm follows his lead."

David stood, his mouth agape. "You're the Wild Falconer?"

"Aye, I've been called that." He didn't remove his gaze from Logan's.

David whistled. "I cannot wait until I can hear more about this."

Will ignored him, still staring at Logan Ramsay. "Do I have your support to free your daughter and wed her? I swear on my honor never to disrespect her, and I will protect her and fight for her until my last breath leaves my body," Will said, staring into Logan's eyes. "I've worked hard to build my skills these past years."

"And what is your strongest ability?"

Gavin glanced at Gregor with a grin, and the two of them answered in unison, "His fists."

Logan quirked his brow.

———◆———

THE GROUP OF MEN HEADED toward the castle two hours later. The crowd was still as rowdy as ever, perhaps even more so because of the amount of ale many of them had imbibed. As they made their way down the streets, Will took a detour into a side shop, purchasing a few daggers of various sizes. He still had his bow and arrows along with his sword, but Maggie wouldn't have been allowed to keep any weapons. While he couldn't carry another bow for her, daggers took up little room, and Maggie was beyond talented with them.

When he emerged from the shop, Logan said, "You're wiser than I thought, MacLerie. You better handfast or there'll be trouble."

Since they were off the main path, Will whistled and glanced up at the sky. Within moments, the two magnificent birds of prey circled over his head. He called to one, "*Trobhad, Stoirm,*" ordering the smaller one to come to him. The smaller bird flew down and landed on his shoulder, but then bounced from one arm to the other. Being a Merlin, he had a more difficult time trusting Will's stability. He hoped the birds would hover nearby.

He set Stoirm off and then returned his attention to Logan. He replied, "I'll do whatever she wishes, find a priest or handfast. 'Twill be her choice." He nodded to Logan, not waiting for a response, and headed down the path toward the castle. He would not let this man interfere with the life he wished to have with Maggie. His woman was compassionate, strong, and intelligent—one of a kind—and he would not risk losing her.

Logan shouted for him to stop, and for a moment, Will thought he'd gone a step too far and the man intended to fight him. Nevertheless, he turned around to look at him. Even in the dark, he could see how this ordeal had aged Logan Ramsay. The older man motioned for him to come closer and guided him to a place they could speak in private. "I want you to know, MacLerie, that I'm only going along with because I trust you and your motivations. I'm aware of your past, and I admire you for handling it the way you have. I also expect the two of you to find your way to Ramsay land within the next moon as husband and wife. I know you'll have to hide, but find a way to let me know she's hale. I want your word on this."

Will nodded. "You have it."

"I don't want my daughter locked up, but I'd rather that than see her neck in a noose. I'm trusting you to save her, William."

"I will, or I'll die trying."

Logan clasped his shoulder and said, "I can't ask for anything more than that."

They rejoined Micheil, David, Gavin, and Gregor. Logan nodded toward Will and said, "Godspeed, the four of you. This is where we leave you. We'll be watching but from a different vantage point. We'll do our best to stir up a distraction." The two brothers stood next to each other.

Micheil reached out to clasp his son's shoulder. "Work together on this, lads," he said.

"Many thanks," Will said. "Now, we must go." He'd memorized the map. He was armed to the teeth. He was ready.

Will spun on his heel and took off toward the castle, running with one goal in mind—to save Maggie. The other lads were fast on his heels.

They passed the entrance into the castle, moving along the curtain wall that encircled it. When they reached a certain point, David grasped Will's shoulder. "This is the spot."

They found an area that wasn't thick with late-night revelers and moved behind the row of houses. As soon as they were out of view, David pointed at a particular stretch of wall. The entire castle had been built in the rocks way above the burgh. The location alone was protection from attack, for the land below the curtain wall of the castle consisted of sections of rock interspersed with steep, uninviting terrain. He pointed to a spot along the wall. "I believe 'tis your best chance of getting over the wall. Guards patrol the entire wall, but with the mob near the center, there won't be many back here. 'Twill be a steep climb, for certes, but I think you can do it. The moon is still full, which should give you enough light, plus once you get closer, you'll see torches along the curtain wall."

"How do you know all this?" Gregor asked.

David shrugged his shoulders. "Boredom mostly. Whenever my brother and I accompanied my parents on one of their visits to the king, they'd be busy with meetings. He and I needed to keep ourselves busy. King Alexander gave us free reign to explore once I hit ten summers. The hard part will be getting to the main part of the keep without being seen, but once you're inside the tower where she's being kept, you'll have no trouble. There are only two staircases to the cellar."

Will took a deep breath and said, "Keep watch for us."

"I pray that Maggie still has her boots or you'll never make it," Gavin said.

"She'll be ready. I promised her I'd come for her tonight. Now I must go."

They all wished him luck before moving back to their assigned positions—Gavin, Gregor, and David hidden in the streets.

Will managed to climb up the steep incline, but once he made it to the wall, he could see two guards patrolling outside a nearby tower. He took a deep breath and threw a rope up over the crenellation and scaled the wall. Fortunately, he wasn't noticed until he was a considerable distance toward the main tower house.

"Halt." One came toward him while another came from behind him. He launched himself at the first, throwing a fist at his jaw to slow him down and then knocking his head against the stone wall. He crumpled without a sound. Will then turned to the second one, spun in a circle to give himself more power, and kicked his leg out, catching the guard square in the face. The man hit the stone wall—a blow that knocked him out.

He didn't have any trouble the rest of the way due to a small fire near the main gates, which had drawn all the guards' attention.

He had a pretty good idea who'd started that fire. He'd thank Logan and Micheil later.

There was definitely more activity closer to the keep, but he waited until the entrance was empty before darting inside. Creeping along the wall, he found the staircase without incident and scrambled down it, peeking down the passageway to the cells before he entered.

The first guard sat on a stool, munching on a piece of bread. "Glad we're not outside with that mob," he shouted to his partner, who sat at the opposite end of the space.

Will came out of the shadows too quickly for the guard

to react. His head slammed back against the stone wall and he fell off the stool, unconscious. The other warrior came at him, struggling to unsheathe his sword, but Will was stronger and faster. He grabbed his sword arm and twisted it, forcing him to drop the weapon, then delivered two blows to the man's belly and two more to his head until he crumpled to the floor.

He passed two empty cells before finding the one that was occupied.

Maggie stood near the door of the cell, peeking out of the bars in the window. "Will, you came for me!" The look on her face made it all worthwhile. When had he ever thought to have such strong feelings for a woman?

CHAPTER EIGHTEEN

MAGGIE THOUGHT SHE HEARD NOISES at the end of the passageway, so she stood and moved over to the grate in the door. She heard a light cry and a thump, and then the guard closest to her flew in front of the window of her cell, desperately trying to unsheathe his sword.

The sounds of struggles and punches reached her, and she said a quick prayer that someone was coming for her. A few moments later, Will's face appeared in front of her, as if her wishes and hopes had summoned him. "Will, you came for me!"

"Did you have any doubts? Hellfire, I've never been so pleased to set eyes on a soul before. Key, where's the key? I didn't find it on either guard."

She pointed to the giant ring on the wall, where she'd watched the guards hang it earlier. The moment Will unlocked the door, she threw herself into his arms with a whimper.

"Hush." He kissed her lips and she melted into him. How she wished he would devour her, but they had to move.

He cupped her face when he ended the kiss. "My plan is to get you away from Edinburgh. Your brother and cousins will protect us until we get outside the gates of the city. Once outside, we'll go to the best caves I know so we can stay hidden."

"Molly?"

"Molly is with a healer and your aunt. Your sire will take care of her. I promised your sire we would marry or handfast. What say you? I promise to use better words when we're safe, but I want you and only you. I believe we were meant to be together." His hand reached up to tuck a few stray hairs behind her ear, then traveled down her neck, sending chills through her everywhere.

"They are the most romantic words I've ever heard. Aye, I'll go anywhere with you, Will MacLerie. I love you."

A smile spread across his face, showing his gorgeous white teeth, and he whispered, "I love you, too. Let's go." He took her hand and headed down the passageway, leading her up the staircase. When he reached the top of the steps, he pulled three daggers out of his sporran and handed them to her. "You may need these."

She tucked them into her belt and nodded. "Lead the way."

They collided with two guards when they exited the main tower. Will took care of one of them while Maggie threw a dagger into the leg of another, dropping him to the ground. They ran past him, and when he opened his mouth to shout, Will swung his fist at the man's jaw to shut him up.

The fire outside the castle lit up the sky, so they had no trouble finding their way to the spot Will had used to climb over the curtain wall. He boosted her ahead of him and they made it over with no trouble. The lads were waiting to join them and they quickly fell in with them— Gavin pausing to say, "Nice you could join us, sister," with a devilish grin—and made haste to the entrance to the burgh.

As they neared the gates, David held something out to Maggie. "Wear this cloak and pull the hood up. You could go down farther and scale the wall to get out of the burgh, but the fire your father started is keeping all the attention away from us. I think we can walk right through if you keep your head down and covered. 'Tis a man's brat, and with your leggings on, you shouldn't arouse any suspicions."

David led them over to the edge, Gavin and Gregor following fast behind them, the four of them doing their best to hide Maggie. Several bucket brigades ran from the river to the burning stables, but the men involved were completely focused on their task. They made it out of the gates without any difficulty, just as her cousin had predicted.

"My sire brought his horse for you. I'll show you," David said. He led them to a horse tied off to the side. "You must go, and do it fast. These two can cover you."

Will did his best to get Maggie on the horse without drawing attention, but it would seem their luck had run out. As soon as she landed atop of the horse, a gust of wind blew her hood off and someone bellowed, "There she is!"

Neither of them turned to look. Will mounted behind her and they took off. Shouts of pain echoed through the air, and she guessed Gavin and Gregor were finding their marks, hidden in the trees. She breathed in deeply, cherishing the night air as if she'd been starved of it for days.

Uncle Micheil's horse was a powerful beast, so what few pursuers had managed to find horses quickly enough to follow them were unable to keep up. It was several hours before Will slowed his horse. When he did, he stopped to listen.

His hand came around Maggie's waist, giving her a light squeeze. "Listen," he whispered.

There were no sounds except for the animals of the forest. Maggie leaned back against Will's chest with a deep sigh. "Are we safe?"

"I think so," he said, kissing her cheek. "There's a hidden cave up ahead. We can spend the night there." He flicked the reins and the horse moved on ahead, nickering as if to say he was glad for the change of pace.

Maggie's fear abated, and she suddenly noticed the heat of Will's body pressed against hers. Her bottom rubbed against the insides of his thighs with each step. A thrill of excitement shot through her, a quivering that did not stop but instead blossomed into pure desire. She wanted to lie with this man, to love him, to cherish him as he did her. He'd risked everything to whisk her out of her prison, going against their king and the King of England.

He led the horse off the main path and through the trees. At first she wondered at their destination, but then she heard the sound of a nearby stream. They could both wash and drink their fill. Will stopped at the burn, and when he helped her down, he slid her slowly down his body until her feet touched the ground…but he didn't let her go.

Maggie wrapped her arms around his neck, lifting her lips to his. His warm, soft lips tasted of her Will, the man she loved. She couldn't stop the small whimper of delight that came out when he ended their kiss.

"Do you wish to freshen up for a wee bit? Then we must go inside and stay there. I think we're safe for the moment, but I don't want to risk aught tonight." He gave her a quick kiss and said, "Go. Take care of your needs, and I'll gather some water and bring my satchel inside. I packed well. I even have ale."

She did as he suggested, then knelt by the stream, washing her hands and throwing water on her face and neck, even down her breasts. That cell had made her feel so dirty. She heard Will behind her, so she glanced around. Her man handed her a linen square and a sliver of soap, charming her even more with his thoughtfulness. "Be quick, but I understand your need after where you were. I'll keep watch."

She sighed with pleasure. Even though the water was cool, it refreshed her as little else could at the moment. She'd tossed her cloak off to the side, but kept her tunic on just to be safe.

When she finished, she turned around and saw Will standing outside of the entrance to the cave, watching her, so she hurried over and launched herself into his arms. "I have not thanked you for what you did."

"Not just me. Your brother and your cousins also helped. Your sire and your uncle set the fire that kept so many distracted." He cupped her face and tugged her inside the cave. "I must keep you safe. Come inside with me. This is our home for the night. I hid the horse over in a spot behind those trees. 'Tis great for grazing and he has water."

She followed him inside, surprised to see that the cave curved. Around the corner and well out of view, she found the special area he'd set up for them, causing her to gasp in surprise. "'Tis beautiful, Will."

There were two candle holders at the outside edges of the space, and a large flat rock in the middle was set like a table. He'd layered furs and plaids off to the side for a bed. On the rock he had set a loaf of fresh bread with cheese, and the flagon of ale.

"How did you do this so quickly?"

He gave her a sheepish grin. "I've stayed here before, so I'd already arranged the rock and the candle holders. I also knew what I planned to do before we left the inn in Edinburgh, so I grabbed the bread, cheese, and ale. I always carry the furs and plaids because I'm used to living outdoors. I even have protective netting for when there are bugs about. Gavin and Gregor held the satchel and the food sack for me. Your brother was worried they wouldn't feed you inside. That's why there's so much cheese."

"'Tis beautiful."

Before they settled, he pulled her close to him, tucking her hands inside his. "I promised your sire and I'm a man of my word. So be patient with me for a moment while I gather my thoughts."

She stood on her tiptoes and kissed his lips with a small smile. "Of course."

A moment later, he cleared his throat and looked into her eyes, the blues and greens of his irises mesmerizing her. "Maggie, you have shown me a world I had never thought possible. A world of sharing and partnership and idealism.

When you're in my arms, there is nowhere I'd rather be. You've given me purpose, something I've lacked for so long. There is naught I'd rather do than wake up with you by my side every morn. Maggie Ramsay, will you do me the honor of becoming my wife as soon as we are able to go before a priest? It would give me great pleasure to handfast with you until we have that opportunity."

Tears misted in her eyes, but they were tears of happiness. "Will, naught would make me happier, so my answer is aye. You have the amazing ability to make me believe in myself." She swiped at her tears and swallowed, doing her best to contain them. "Together, I feel we're invincible. But I must ask you a question. Are you still willing to marry me if we must leave Scotland? What if my sire cannot set things to rights and I must stay in hiding? Who knows where he might send me? He has many friends in many places."

"Then I'll hide with you. I am still wanted for murder in these parts. Are you sure you want an outlaw as your husband?"

Maggie wrapped her hands around his neck and whispered, "Aye. I love you and will go anywhere with you." His lips descended on hers and she parted her lips for him, wanting everything he could give her. The kiss was demanding and hot, a kiss of love and desire. An irrepressible need overtook her, driving her to an edge that was new to her, as he continued to angle his mouth over hers.

"Are you sure you want this as much as I do?" he rasped, pulling back slightly.

"Aye, make me yours."

He moved over to blow one candle out, but then asked, "Do you mind if I leave one burning? I want to see all of you, feel you against my skin."

"Aye. 'Tis what I want, too." She reached for the hem of her tunic, but her hands quivered so much he had to help her. Then she helped him with his leine, letting her hands trail across his musculature and the planes of his abdomen toward his breeches.

"Your boots?"

They both removed their boots, then her leggings and the rest of his clothes until they stood unadorned in front of each other.

He whispered, "You bind your breasts?"

She nodded. "Will you help me? 'Tis easier to shoot and run with them bound."

He helped her unwind the linen until her breasts broke free. "Maggie, my God, you're beautiful." He reached to cup her breasts, but then paused, "May I?"

Of course, Will would ask her first. How she adored him. Somehow hearing him call her beautiful made it acceptable. It made her *want* to be beautiful. "Aye, I want you to touch me as I wish to touch you."

They explored each other's body in the dark, both their hands and their lips traveling in new areas. Will stopped her and said, "Your hair? May I unbraid it?"

She nodded and spun around, surprised at her own boldness. She wasn't embarrassed about her body in front of him. It felt right, as if they'd been made for each other to enjoy. She pulled out the leather ties and pins, but he stilled her hands when she attempted to unwind the plait.

His hands massaged her scalp as he worked his hands into the thickness of her hair, each touch feeling like the softest of caresses. She moaned lightly, tipping her head in the direction of his ministrations, allowing him to control her movement. Had anything ever felt this good?

His lips fell to her shoulder, kissing a hot trail across her back that made her shiver while his hands moved down to caress her bottom, the softest touch possible feathering across the round globes before moving around to the front of her body, cupping her breasts and pulling her back against him.

His erection pressed against her backside, and she felt the

sudden urge to touch his hardness. She pivoted, reaching for him, shocked at the heat of his shaft, the velvety surface calling her other hand to him. He moaned and showed her how to move her hands the way he liked it, giving her a sense of power unlike anything she'd experienced before.

"Maggie," he panted. "Lie with me."

She nodded and he scooped her up into his arms. Squealing with delight, she kissed the stubble on his neck. When he settled her down on the furs and lowered himself next to her, he said, "You know…"

"Aye, I know 'twill hurt, but I'm ready. I want this."

CHAPTER NINETEEN

WILL WAS CERTAIN HE'D DIED and gone to heaven. Maggie's passion stirred him to new heights. He moved his fingers to the vee between her legs, seeking her liquid heat. When he found her slick and ready for him, he moaned and kissed her again, his body reaching a fevered pitch that drove him forward. Want consumed him, but he knew he'd never get enough.

His hands sought her curves again and he moved over her, settling himself between her thighs. "Guide me, love." His hand moved to her breast, teasing her nipple to a taut peak as she reached for him, spreading her legs wide to accommodate him.

He took over then, teasing her entrance until he was covered with her juices, allowing him to slip into her until her barrier stopped him. While his plan had been to take this slowly, his need overtook him. He grasped her hips and plunged inside.

She cried out and gripped his shoulders. He froze at once, whispering into her ear, "I'm so sorry. I should have gone slower. I'm not verra experienced."

"Nay, 'tis not so bad, but please wait. I hear it subsides."

"It will, I promise. I won't move until you tell me to." He kissed her forehead, then her cheek and her lips, balancing his weight on his elbows.

She moved against him, just a touch, but it was sheer torture. "Sweeting, you are so tantalizing to me that if you move, 'tis harder for me to keep still."

"Then don't. I want you. I want *this*, Will. Try and see

if 'tis better." Molly had told her all about the first time, how it hurt terribly but then felt wonderful after a few moments. She wanted the wonderful, vowing to ignore the slight pinch that still remained.

He pulled back and then eased into her again, causing her to spread her legs wider. "More, Will. It feels better."

He pulsed into her with a rhythm that caught her, and she joined him, managing to leverage herself so his thrusts moved deeper inside her. After a few more strokes, she knew she was on the precipice of something, but what?

"Tell me what to do, Will. I need something more," she panted out.

He reached down between them and touched a spot that made something inside her explode. Her entire being shattered into a thousand pieces and she shouted his name at the same moment he roared out his satisfaction.

When she was able to think again, she caressed the back of his neck, doing her best to calm her breathing. His panting matched her own and she smiled. "You were pleased as much as I was?"

"More," he gasped, rolling onto his side and taking her with him, settling her head on his shoulder.

She fell asleep moments later, the sheer exhaustion of the day taking over.

———◆———

WILL WOKE UP WITH A start, thinking he'd heard something. Maggie was still sound asleep, so he managed to sneak away without waking her. He moved to the front of the cave to stand in the opening, listening carefully, but nothing appeared amiss. Though it was dark, he knew the area, so he stepped outside the cave to make sure all was well. After making his way back to their horse to feed him some oats and give him a pat, he stepped back inside.

He returned to his wife, his home, his everything.

He couldn't imagine being any happier…well, unless they were both free. Maggie opened her eyes and whispered, "Is aught wrong?"

"Nay. Go back to sleep. 'Tis the middle of the night. I checked outside and there's no one there. We're well hidden." He settled back onto the furs next to her.

"Where do we go from here?" she whispered, rolling onto her side. Propping her head on one hand, she settled her free one on his chest, playing with the dark hairs there.

His gaze caught hers and he said, "Wherever you want to go. I have an idea, see if you agree with me."

"I'm sure I will."

He set his hand behind his head and said, "I think the first thing we should do is go back to my grandsire's. I don't think the king's men would think to look for you there, and I'm sure my grandpapa can give us more information about what is going on. Your sire said if Brenna hadn't yet taken the lassies home, he would bring them to Edinburgh to present evidence against Baines. He sent Cailean back to see. The only way we'll know is if we return to ask. We should be able to make it there by nightfall."

"Aye," she said with a smile. "That would be my first choice. I'd like to see how the lassies are. Beatris was in such bad shape. Maybe I should wish they were taken to Edinburgh, but I'd rather they were with Aunt Brenna. They need stability and the chance to be children again. She's wonderful."

His gaze caught hers. "That's my lass. Putting others' needs ahead of her own. I'm sure they will be gone."

She nodded, playing with one braid she'd recently plaited. "Aye, but at least your grandsire can tell us how they fared. I wonder how the wee pup is doing with Simone."

Will reached over to play with her braid. "I'm sure Angus has enjoyed all four lassies. We'll have to train him when we have the chance, and he needs to fatten up as much as Beatris does."

"Don't you think they'll be good for one another?"

He nodded. "Aye, for certes. As for the other matter, I don't think we can make any decisions until we find out what happened in Edinburgh."

"Aye," she said. "Then what?"

"My guess is we'll have to wait another sennight before we travel to Ramsay land."

"Please don't forget our most important mission."

He turned his head to gaze into her eyes.

"I'm going after Randall Baines. I won't settle until that man is either dead or stripped of his earldom. He's a monster."

———◆———

THE NEXT MORN, MAGGIE WOKE up to see Will sitting on the rock, digging something out of his satchel. When he found it, his eyes lit up. "Aye, I do have several left."

Maggie sat up, covering herself with a warm plaid in the cool air. "What did you find?"

"A wee treat for my bride. I saved some hazelnuts from last fall, so you can have some to break your fast, then I'll take you to the small pool behind the cave so we can both clean up before we move on. There are no pools again until we reach my grandsire's area."

"Do you think 'tis safe?"

"Aye. I think most will have aching heads this morn from all the whisky they imbibed last eve." He smashed the hazelnuts in front of the cave, glancing through the area as he did so. Maggie stood behind him wrapped in a plaid, her own gaze scanning the area. He handed her the sweet meat and she nibbled on the succulent treat, sighing with pleasure. "Have you many more?"

"Back at Grandpapa's I have a basketful, but this is all I had in my satchel. There's more cheese and a few oatcakes. Once we move farther away from Edinburgh, I'll hunt and roast something for dinner." He took a long, lingering look at her before adding, "I'll take you to the pool when you're ready."

She savored the hazelnuts, then grabbed her clothing. She had only one clean undergarment that she'd stashed inside her binding, something she often did.

Will took her by the hand and led the way to the pool.

It wasn't a large one but it was semi-private because it was surrounded by thick greenery on three sides. She shed the plaid and slipped into the water quickly, giving a slight gasp when the cool water covered her. Will slipped in beside her, handing her a sliver of soap. "If you need help, I'd be glad to be of assistance." He waggled his brow at her, but she just smiled. They were both distracted by all the noises, the fear of being caught fresh on their minds.

All of a sudden, Will stilled.

"What is it?" She hurriedly finished her ablutions, dipping her hair under to wash it before they were to leave. Though she couldn't suds it up well, at least she was able to wash out the cobwebs she'd run into in their escape from the castle.

Will climbed out and donned his clothing, staring into the air.

"Will? You're scaring me." She rinsed her hair, set the soap on the rock and climbed out.

"Here, use my tunic to dry yourself. 'Tis clean. Then dress quickly." He stared into the sky again, and to her relief, a broad smile crossed his face. He reached into his satchel and pulled out a rough piece of cloth, wrapping it around his forearm.

He whistled and a large bird circled the air above them.

"Will? Do you recognize that bird? Is it your falcon?" Once she was dressed, she hid behind him, but he set her off to the side before he held his arm up.

The falcon circled two more times before it swooped in toward them, landing on a tree branch not far from them.

"Greetings, my friend. I'm glad for your presence. We may need you. Maggie, you remember Sealgar. He's quite the hunter." He tipped his head closer to his friend. "Maggie is now my wife, Sealgar. You must watch over her, too."

Will moved over to the branch and put his forearm close to the bird, which climbed onto his arm without hesitation.

"Will! How did you ever get him to do that?" she asked in bafflement. Though a couple of her cousins had a way with wild animals, she'd never seen a falcon that hadn't been raised in captivity act quite like that.

"Och, so you'd like the full story of my pets? You know I lived in the outdoors traveling from cave to cave for a long time. One day I found this poor beast lying on the ground with a wound in his breast. It wasn't a deep one, but it affected his ability to fly. So I took him home to grandpapa and we covered him with his special poultice. He stayed outside our cottage for a few days until he was able to fly again. We fed him fish and he accepted us. After that, he often followed me on my travels…almost like he wanted to keep an eye on me. And where is Stoirm, my fine feathered friend?"

Sealgar let out a loud call, and another falcon appeared, flying directly toward them and settling on the branch. This one had a light-blue plumage the likes of which she'd never seen up close. Will explained, "This is Stoirm. I found him not far from our home with a broken wing, which I did my best to repair. Quite a happy coincidence that it happened when Sealgar was still healing."

"They're beautiful, Will. The blue plumage on Stoirm is quite stunning. You have special talents."

He waggled his brow at her and said, "You have yet to see all of my special talents." Sealgar squawked and took off in flight, Stoirm doing the same.

Will's face turned serious, his gaze again searching the area. "Come," he said a moment later, "let's get moving. I packed everything up, but we should leave. I don't like the way the falcons are acting. They sense things before I do."

They maneuvered their way back to the cave, but Will slowed when they neared the mouth. Sealgar stayed in the area, making all kinds of noise that made Maggie uneasy. "Do you think the falcon sees someone?"

Will took her hand and darted around a tree. He let go of her and shoved her backward, shouting, "Run!"

Three men headed toward them, two on horseback and one on foot. The one on the horse said, "You go after the girl. She won't be able to run that fast. Get her!"

CHAPTER TWENTY

———◆———

MAGGIE LEAPED OVER A ROCK and ran as fast as she could, darting in and out, trying to make sure she didn't get caught in the eye by a branch.

Her pursuer taunted her all the way. "You think you can outrun me? We'll see. You're just a silly lass."

She ran through the trees, swinging branches back in the hopes of hitting her attacker in the face. In the distance, she heard the clash of swords, so Will had to be battling the other two. She said a quick prayer for help. She glanced backward to see if the man was still following her, and to her surprise, he was gaining on her.

She and Molly had always been fast runners, but this man was equally quick.

"There's a large bounty on your head, Ramsay. I'm taking you in, and it'll be my pleasure to teach you a few lessons before we get there."

Her feet pounded over the stones and shrubbery, cutting her in places because she couldn't choose her path. If she could only get a good distance ahead of him, she could fling a dagger at him since she had one in her boot. She ran around a large group of rocks, surprised to see he had disappeared.

It wasn't a good sign, but she continued on, her chest feeling as though it were about to explode, gasping for air. Fear constricted her throat; she was not held back by any inability to run. She came around a tree and ran right into the bastard.

"Hah! I know this land better than you." He struggled with her and she kicked him several times, which only served to infuriate him. He threw one punch at her but missed. She did her best to grab her dagger, but she couldn't reach it. Tossing her to the ground, he climbed on top of her, slapping her once.

"Foolish bitch. Just give up. You'll never beat me." He threw his weight across her, pinning her to the ground, squeezing the breath from her.

She tried again for her dagger, but her reach was a little bit short. Out of nowhere, a small falcon swooped down to peck him in the head. He bellowed at the bird, but the blessed creature had moved the bastard enough so she could grab her weapon. She unsheathed it and swung, catching him square in the back. He rolled off her with a shout and she pulled the dagger back and stabbed him straight in his belly. He didn't move, his eyes rolling back in his head. She wiped her hands in a pile of leaves, though there was little blood on them. She just had to get rid of the feel of him, so she dragged them across an area thick with moss and then ran to the stream to stick them—and the dagger—in the water.

She had no idea if the man was dead or alive, and didn't want to know. Her sire's instructions had always been that she should defend herself in any attack, whatever it took. But if these were the king's men, would she be hanged or imprisoned for killing or maiming one of them? What was someone to do when they were attacked?

She raced back toward the cave where she'd left Will. The sound of swordfight had ended, though she was a distance away.

Then she heard his voice. "Maggie, Maggie, where are you?"

She broke into a sob, unable to speak, but as soon as she saw him, she leaped into his arms.

He kissed her hard on the mouth and she gasped at the pleasure of being in his arms again.

"I was so frightened. Are you all right? He did not harm you in any way?" Will, frantic with worry, touched her everywhere.

"Nay. Make love to me, Will. I want to be sure I remember us together forever, just in case anything happens. Please?"

"Now?" he whispered.

"Aye, now."

He found a spot far away from where they'd been attacked, lay her down on the soft moss, and the two of them scrambled to undress. Finally free, their bodies melded together, and he plunged into her with one thrust. She gasped and he stilled. "Did I hurt you?"

"Nay." She grasped his buttocks and pulled him toward her, setting a fast pace, and he joined her. "Do not stop. I want you." Maggie was possessed by a frenzy that overtook her every thought. She couldn't explain her fear, but she wished to remember their love forever.

Their lovemaking was wild and frantic. She scored his back with her nails in her urgency to climax. His gaze locked on hers and all she could think was how much she loved him. They moved together with a rhythm that brought her to tears because it was so beautiful, this amazing act of moving as one, until they both climaxed at the same time. He shouted her name and she was unable to scream, unable to speak.

When they finished, he clutched her to him, and she buried her face in his chest, still panting and crying as he kissed the top of her head. "I love you so much, Maggie."

"I love you, too, Will. I'm so frightened for us."

———◆———

RANDALL BAINES CURSED AS SOON as he climbed off his horse in the courtyard of his Edinburgh castle. How the hell had this escapade turned into such a disaster? Now he was forbidden to leave Edinburgh. There was only one reason for all his problems.

Young Maggie Ramsay, all grown up.

The little bitch had started the entire episode back in Wingate. She'd kidnapped one of his kitchen maids and injured his housekeeper and two of his guards. No matter that they were fine now—she owed him for causing him so much trouble. He'd had to lie about their supposed death just to convince the foolish Scottish king to imprison her.

Then the bitch had interfered with his most valued cargo yet. She'd stolen the two surviving girls, not to mention the pain she'd inflicted on him. Hell, he'd nearly passed out from her blows. He'd barely been able to speak by the time the ship had docked for his cargo. Fortunately, the captain of the ship hadn't bellowed too much over the loss of the girls, but it had cost Baines a considerable amount of coin.

He wiped the sweat from his brow as he climbed the steps to his small keep, swearing again just because he was still in Scotland. He wanted Maggie Ramsay hung and then her head placed on a spike for all to see in the middle of Edinburgh. He'd sent a message to King Edward *and* King Alexander.

His captain followed him inside the hall, waiting until his master sat down at a trestle table with a drink before he gave him the latest news.

"What is it, Granville? It better be good news for a change."

"It isn't, my lord. Maggie Ramsay has escaped from the castle."

He bolted out of his chair, sending it flying backwards with a bang. "What? How does someone escape the royal castle, especially from that hill in Edinburgh? Micheil and Logan Ramsay had a hand in this, I swear, or perhaps that bold bitch, Diana."

"They didn't. Word is she was rescued by a man dressed in all black. The man who was with her at Wingate—the Wild Falconer."

"That man's her accomplice, he was with her at the firth. When they find him, I'll see him strung up, too. Those two have caused me nothing but trouble." He thought of what his contact would say when he found out his promised cargo had not been delivered. Baines feared he may never return for his next shipment. One more, he just needed one more.

He hadn't heard the door open, but his marshal walked inside, followed by two men. Ah, Aldus and Elric Bullard had returned. He waved for them all to join him at the table. "You tell me good news. Granville has none."

"Sorry, my lord. I heard the end of the conversation, and everything I've heard verifies the truth of his statement. Will MacLerie is the Wild Falconer and is also wanted for the death of the brother of the MacEwan laird. They said he killed the man two years ago for taking his mother's life for witchery. He's an expert at escape. The Scottish king has been after him for two years. It's doubtful they'll find them."

"If they've been searching for him for years, I have to agree. They'll never locate them. Perhaps I need to adjust my thinking." He rubbed the scruff of his beard. "I should have sent men after them immediately."

"You'd have lost them. A group of reivers tried to overtake them for the reward, but they're nowhere to be found."

"I'll accept it as a lost cause. No matter. There are plenty of other Scots who could serve my purposes. I'll have to plan carefully." He sat back down and set his boots up on the closest chair, crossing his arms in thought.

Elric said, "Wait until you hear our news. There's talk of other suppliers involved in the same type of cargo as you. We haven't uncovered it completely, but if your contact refuses to use your services again, you may have another option."

Randall felt a smile spread across his face as the comment settled in. Yes, they'd caught his attention. "All right.

I want you to find out all you can about this operation. When you have more news, come back. And don't bother me until you have actual news, not rumors. I want names."

His marshal asked, "I thought you'd decided not to pursue Maggie Ramsay, my lord?"

"I've another victim in mind. I should have thought of this long ago."

"Which one?" deVere asked. "Shall we go after the person now?"

"No." He clasped his hands behind his head and leaned back in his chair. "This one will be all mine."

CHAPTER TWENTY-ONE

———✦———

THEY'D PACKED UP THEIR BELONGINGS and headed out as quickly as possible. The rest of the day had been uneventful. Maggie was amazed at how happy she felt despite the danger they were in. Every time Will leaned down to kiss her cheek just to let her know he was thinking of her, her heart swelled.

She'd had no idea this kind of love could be hers. How wonderful life would be if only they could live on Ramsay land with her clan, have a family of their own.

"What are you thinking about, love?" he whispered.

She glanced at him over her shoulder. "About how happy I am and how wonderful it could be if we weren't considered outlaws by our king."

"Aye, 'tis true, but I have faith in your sire. I've heard many a tale about the mighty Logan Ramsay and his wife, Gwyneth. Your sire will straighten this out, and if he has any trouble, I'm certain Clan Grant would bring their massive legion of warriors down to Edinburgh to help. I look forward to meeting your Uncle Alex someday. 'Tis said he's still the best swordsman in all the land."

"Uncle Alex is wonderful. I think you may be as tall as him, though his shoulders are much broader."

"I'm still working on that," he said with a chuckle.

"My cousin Loki is a talented swordsman, mayhap as good as Uncle Alex, and my sire thinks Cailean could battle either of them. Of course, my mother thinks differently."

"How so?"

"She believes Uncle Alex's youngest son will take the

reputation. He's almost as tall as his father and he's just twenty. She thinks he's still growing."

"How old is your brother?"

"He's ten and eight, the same as Gregor, David, and our Grant cousins Roddy and Braden."

"Och. You have a large family."

"I know. 'Tis most wonderful. I'd be quite sad if I were never to see them again."

"If all else fails, we can go deep into the Highlands, hide near your cousins. They would allow us on Grant land, would they not?"

She nodded. "Aye. You would willingly go that far?"

He stopped the horse and turned her sideways to look at him. "I've told you, I go where you go. My life is wherever you are. If we must hide, then we shall hide. I'm not averse to living in caves for the rest of my life, as long as you're by my side. However, I hope someday you'll be carrying our son or daughter, and then I would rather that we not be alone in a cave when the bairn arrives."

The man humbled her. All she could say was, "I love you, Will." But it didn't seem like enough. This man made her feel strong, beautiful, loved, and he asked for nothing in return but her love.

It was almost dusk when they arrived at his grandsire's cottage. They hid the horse under the lean-to the older man had built for protection in the patch of trees immediately behind the building. "Once we talk with grandsire, I'll brush your uncle's horse down. He's a fine animal." The beast whinnied in response, as if to agree with him. "Aye, I'll bring you oats in a wee bit. Graze and drink for a few minutes." He patted the animal and took her hand, leading her inside the hut.

"Grandpapa? You are here?" he called out.

He knocked on the door quietly before opening it, only to be surprised by a small form that barreled directly toward him. Simone hugged first him and then Maggie, crying with delight. "You are well, both of you? A very big Ramsay man came to stay with us. I heard him talking with one of his guards, Maggie. You were locked up, and it sounds like 'tis all my fault…"

Ah, so Cailean had come and gone. She'd suspected as much. There were no signs of the other lasses they'd saved, so perhaps they'd been brought back to Ramsay land.

Maggie knelt down to bring her face level with Simone's. "Nay, lassie, not because of you but because of the Earl of Wingate. He told many lies, saying I killed three of his people. I don't believe any of them died from the injuries we inflicted on them." She took Simone's hand and led her over to where Will's grandsire sat at the hearth.

"William. You are hale?" his grandsire asked.

"Aye, we are fine. Grandpapa, Maggie and I handfasted and we will marry as soon as we are able."

The older man threw his arms over his head with a wide smile. "You have made me proud and your mother would be happy to hear you've married. Maggie's a fine lassie, and I wish you much happiness. Come, sit, and tell me all about your escapades. I was worried about you two. Before I forget, the big lad came back looking for the lassies, but Maggie's aunt had already come for them. I had a lovely chat with her. She's quite enchanting and has a quick mind, that one. Beatris needed someone like her—a motherly figure. She should do well with your clan, Maggie."

Will said, "Answer me one question, Grandpapa. Then I must take care of the fine horse we borrowed. I hope you have some oats left. He deserves it for getting us away from Edinburgh safely."

"Your question?"

"Has anyone come looking for us?"

The older man sighed and stroked his beard. "Aye. Besides our Ramsay visitors, the king's men have also been here. They asked for you by name, saying you were wanted for murder of the MacEwan brother. I argued with them, but they would not listen. I'm afraid you'll need to stay in hiding."

"My thanks, Grandpapa." He leaned over to kiss Maggie and said, "After we take care of the horse and refill our supplies, we must keep moving. We should probably sleep in the cave." He left to take care of the horse.

"But where will you go?" Simone asked, turning to Maggie.

"We're going after Randall Baines," Maggie said without hesitation. "If he tells the truth, I'll be free. And even if he doesn't, we must make sure he doesn't hurt any more young girls. Tell me more about your sister and the other lassies."

"Beatris is much better. Your aunt came and stayed with us overnight. Then they left for Ramsay land with ten guards. Geva and Emma and Beatris went with them. The wee ones insisted on taking the puppy with them." She swiped at her tears. "My sister was happy sitting on Aunt Brenna's lap. She said we could call her Auntie. Beatris is only five summers. I'm old enough not to need someone like a mama, but she…she loved Auntie Brenna."

"Aye, the lass never moved away from her," Will's grandsire said. "She needs a mother figure to help her heal. Geva and Emma were happy to go with her, especially when Brenna told them about all the young lassies in your clan. I also explained to Simone that wee Angus needs to grow strong before he'll be able to travel as far as Edinburgh. The poor pup was starved for certes."

"Aye, they'll be well taken care of there, but why did you not go with them, Simone?" Maggie asked.

"Because I wish to travel with you. Cailean returned to bring all of us to Edinburgh, but when he found out I was the only one left, he wasn't sure what to do. I told him I was willing to come along, but only with you, so he left, though a few guards stayed behind to protect us."

"Where are they?" Maggie asked Will's grandsire.

"They're out patrolling. I told them which area to watch. The two guards Brenna left with us are closer." The old man stroked his beard for a bit. "Not to interfere, but are you sure you wish to bring this lassie with you to Edinburgh? You could have a rough journey."

Simone shook her head stubbornly. "Randall Baines tried to kill my sister. He needs to pay for what he did, and I wish to tell our king what a bad man he is." She swiped at her tears again.

"What do you think, Maggie?" the old man asked.

Maggie thought for a moment, pleased when the door opened and Will returned. Turning to him, she said, "We're discussing taking Simone back with us to Edinburgh with us. Your grandsire wonders if it is safe for her. What do you think?"

"You might be a better judge, Maggie," he said. "I did not hear all you discussed with the king."

Flustered by the thought that popped into her head, she said, "I don't know your name other than Grandpapa."

He waved a crooked hand at her. "Call me Nevin. Nevin MacLerie. Someday I hope you'll call me Grandpapa, but we've only just met."

She paused, then said, "Nevin, I understand your concern, but I think the king needs to hear from someone like Simone, someone who has experienced the earl's cruelty directly. It has been a long time since I lived at Wingate."

"Please? You can dress me like a lad and call me Simon," the lassie pressed.

"Are you sure?" Maggie asked, scooping her loose hair back across her neck. "Wouldn't he remember you from working in the kitchens at Wingate? I don't want the earl to recognize you."

Simone shook her head. "He never came into the kitchens. If we saw him outside, we ran and hid. Everyone was afraid of him."

Maggie's fury at the man came back to her with a roar.

Bastard. Though she hated the thought of endangering Simone, she also knew what it was to wish for vengeance. "Do you think you can sleep in a cave?"

The lass nodded vehemently. "I promise to be good. I can help."

Will nodded. "Aye, I think you can."

His grandpapa cut in, "Why don't you two spend the night in the cave and make your plans? Simone can stay with me one more night, then you can take her with you on the morrow."

"Must I?" Simone asked.

Grandpapa winked at Maggie. "Please don't make me spend the night alone," he said to the wee lass. "One more night and you may go. They are newly wed and need some privacy."

"All right. One more night, then we go after Randall Baines." Simone's eyes carried a fury not unlike her own.

———◆———

WILL OPENED HIS EYES THE next morn, looking at his wife lying beside him. She was a most beautiful woman, and the ferocity of her passion had surprised him. Making love to Maggie was a new experience each time because her sexual appetite was as voracious as his own.

She opened one eye to peer at him as he sat up.

He leaned over to kiss her forehead. "Good morn to you, gorgeous."

"Must we leave so soon? I could stay another day or two here. This cave is as well stocked as your cottage."

"Aye, but I suspect Simone will not feel the same."

She sighed. "Aye, I won't rest either until this is done." Shifting to her knees, she threw her arms around his neck and kissed him sweetly, her breasts pressing against him. They both slept with naught on, wrapped in each other's arms.

"If you wish to go soon, you'd better cover up those beautiful mounds or I'll not be able to keep my hands away." He glanced down at his growing erection. "See what you do to me?"

She chuckled and stood, wrapping a plaid around her delectable body. "We must go." She paused for a moment, shifting from one foot to the other.

"What's wrong?" he asked. "Did I hurt you?"

"Nay," she replied. "I am a little sore, but I couldn't get enough of you last night, so 'tis not your fault."

"I'll remember that. Three times is too much for you in one night. There are other ways we can satisfy each other that won't rub you raw."

Her eyes widened. "There are? Oh, I cannot wait to learn more."

They headed down from the hill to the cottage after fetching some fresh water from a nearby spring, but Will stopped abruptly, hiding her behind him. "There are horses and many of them. Who the hell could it be?"

She peeked over his shoulder. "Gavin and Gregor," she squealed. She ran in front of him, causing his heart to leap into this throat.

He stopped and pulled her back. "You know not who else is with them. They could have been followed. There are more than three horses. Is one your sire's?" If he had to watch her be tied up again and thrown into that dirty cell, he'd not survive it. She belonged with him. They belonged together.

She hesitated, his words apparently sinking in. "I don't know the other horses. Who could it be?"

"Promise me you'll stay here? I'll peek through the window, move the fur enough to see."

Before he had the chance to move, the door opened and Simone popped out. "I'll find them. They said we'd be leaving soon."

A man as tall as Will stepped out of the cottage, his hair

dark as night, followed by a lad with golden hair. Maggie gasped in surprise. "Connor? Roddy?"

Ah, so these were the Grant cousins she'd told him about.

The dark-haired man smiled. "Maggie? Come closer. We came to help."

She tugged on Will's hand and ran forward. This time he let her. "Will, these are my cousins. Alex Grant's son Connor and Robbie Grant's son Roddy."

The blond man, Roddy, said, "Braden's inside with Gavin and Gregor."

David emerged from the woods just then, a wide grin splitting his face. "You two made it, I see. Are you married yet?"

They all squeezed back into the cottage so they could speak privately.

"Hellfire, Will, I've never seen so many giant lads in my life," his grandsire said, shaking his head. Will could tell he was secretly delighted to have so many visitors. "Lassie, you have some big cousins."

"Where have you two been?" Gavin asked, clapping Will on the back. He hadn't ventured outside with the others. "Need I ask? Let me guess. You handfasted and spent the night alone in the woods, dabbling with *nature*." The way the last word came out caused the group of lads to burst into laughter.

Maggie wouldn't be shamed for loving her husband, but before Will could open his mouth to say anything, she replied, "Dabble we did, and this is my husband, Will MacLerie, for those of you who haven't yet met him. My question is why are you all here?"

Will, Maggie, Gavin, and David settled around the table while the others settled on stools or stood.

"Torrian sent word of your troubles," Connor said, "with details of the group in Edinburgh, so we volunteered to help Gavin, Gregor, and David. We're all cousins. We need to stick together. Besides, tales of the Wild Falconer even reached us on Grant land."

Roddy said, "I couldn't wait to leave. 'Twas a long winter. Tell us more about your travels, Will. Did you truly kill a wolf with your bare hands?"

Gavin and Gregor stared at him in awe to see his response. Will acted quite humble. He replied, "Not quite true." That was all they needed to know. He wasn't going to glorify an act he'd rather not think about.

Gregor stared at him, wide-eyed. "Nay? Tell them what happened, Gavin."

Gavin, always the jester, was only too happy to edge his way into the conversation. "Mayhap 'tis not completely true, but I do recall the time a wolf flew at you. 'Twas before you'd learned much with your bow."

"Aye, and your cousin threw his dagger at the wolf, saving me." Will shrugged his shoulders.

"Huh," Gavin looked at Gregor. "Cousin, is that what you recall?"

The other lad chuckled. "Not exactly. True, I threw my dagger, but it did not stop the beast. He paused for a moment, narrowed his gaze, and launched himself at your neck with his jaws wide open."

"Och, 'tis what I recall, too," Gavin added, his face lighting up. "And you grabbed the beast by the neck and twisted until he croaked." He bugged his eyes and stuck out his tongue, mimicking the wolf.

Gregor said, "I think he beat his head on the boulder a bit."

Connor's expression turned serious. "Sounds true to me, Will. I bow to you."

All faces turned toward Will, including Maggie's. He couldn't think of anything to say. He couldn't deny the truth, but the beast had come at him with a dagger in its flank.

Fortunately, one of the cousins saved him. Braden, who seemed more serious than the others, said, "Whatever we can do to assist you, we will. Gladly."

Will was overwhelmed by their offer. With their help, he hoped they could indeed find a way out of this mess. He squeezed his wife's hand and said, "We graciously accept. I'll not allow Maggie to be imprisoned again. Could we put our heads together and come up with a plan to end the reign of the wicked Earl of Wingate?"

"With pleasure," Roddy said. The others nodded their agreement.

CHAPTER TWENTY-TWO

———

A FEW HOURS LATER, THEIR PLAN was set. They would depart in two hours.

Aside from Will's grandsire, all of them were going to Edinburgh together.

Maggie held her hand out to Simone and said, "Come, we'll go outside."

They headed to the small, well-hidden waterfall that Will had shown her the previous night. She pulled out the sliver of soap she kept tucked in the pocket sewn inside her tunic, then stripped down and stepped into the water. "Come with me. 'Twill be a while before we can wash again."

Simone followed, giggling as she stepped into the stream's cool water.

Maggie washed her face, then said, "I need your promise before we take you along. You must not do aught without checking with me first."

Simone stared up at her, the innocence in her gaze nearly causing Maggie to mist up. "I promise, Maggie. You saved me and my sister. I wish to stay with you forever. I'll be good. I love you and Will." She swiped at her own tears.

"Simone, we will not desert you, but I need your word that you'll listen to Will and me…even if you don't understand our reasoning. 'Tis too dangerous for you to come otherwise." All of a sudden, she understood all the times her parents had treated her like a child. They'd only been trying to protect her, just as she felt driven to protect this wee lassie.

"I promise."

"Good. You must be careful, but I believe we have a sound plan."

Will's voice carried across the fur trees. "Maggie?"

Simone squealed, jumping out of the water. "Stay away!" she cried out.

Maggie had no inclination to cover herself around her husband, but she remembered feeling exactly like Simone did.

"Sister, let's get moving." Gavin's voice caused her to jump almost as high as Simone had.

"We'll be right there. Don't come any closer, either of you." She climbed out and helped Simone into the new lads' clothing Will's grandpapa had given them. Then she dressed herself. When they finished, they followed the path back to the cottage. Maggie came to an abrupt stop as they entered the clearing.

It was an image that would leave a lasting impression on her. Standing next to the cottage was Will and her brother and cousins, all of them dressed in dark clothing. They looked like outlaws.

Grandpapa stood in front of the doorway, taking it all in with a grin on his face. "They are quite impressive, are they not, lassie? You have quite a band of cousins there."

Indeed, she did. "No plaids?"

"Nothing to identify ourselves," David said with a nod. "'Tis not uncommon in Edinburgh. There are plenty who don't identify with a clan. We carry our plaids in our satchels. For now, we dress like your husband."

"Many thanks to you all," she said, wishing to go around and hug each one individually.

"You can thank us when this is over," Connor said. "I think we should move now, get ourselves in place at dusk. We have much to do when we arrive in Edinburgh."

Will lifted Maggie onto the horse Aunt Brenna had left for her, then settled Simone in front of her. "Mount up, lads. 'Tis time for us to settle this once and for all."

Grandsire stood on the stoop and waved them off. "God-speed."

They rode for a couple of hours before reaching the outskirts of Edinburgh, and then Simone led them back to the earl's castle. The others waited at the end of the road while Maggie and Simone—Simon, as she now appeared—snuck closer to the castle. The lassie climbed up a tree to get a better view of the situation.

"What do you see?" Maggie asked.

"Naught," Simone said. "There's no movement at all. I only see two guards at the gate."

"Then we shall move on to the second plan. Climb down and I'll hide over there while you approach the guards. I'll cover you, do not worry. I have plenty of daggers."

Simone climbed down, then took the piece of rolled parchment out of her tunic. She bravely marched over to the two guards and announced, "I have a missive for the Earl of Wingate. Is he in residence?"

Maggie listened carefully to the conversation, ready to act as soon as she was needed.

"What's your name?" one of the guards asked.

"Simon. I have this for the earl." She held the missive in front of her. One of the guards reached for it, but she tugged it back. "Is he in residence? If not I'll seek him elsewhere."

"He's not here. He's at the royal castle."

The other guard turned to glare at the first. "Are you daft? Just say he's here and take the missive."

Simone said, "My thanks. I'll go there." She flew down the path before either one could grab her.

"You there! Halt!"

She ignored them and ran back toward the end of the road. Maggie stayed to see if they would pursue her, but they didn't. One of them grabbed his ale and sat on the ground. "Fine with me if she goes to the castle. They'll not let her inside to speak with him."

"Not when he's with the kings and the Ramsays. He'll never step outside."

As soon as they turned their heads, Maggie raced back toward the group, a huge smile on her face. Simone had already rejoined the others. She motioned for everyone to mount and move out of hearing distance, then addressed them as a group.

"Did I do good?" Simone asked.

"That was perfect. Baines is at the royal castle with the Ramsays and the kings, according to the guards. Sounds like both of them are there."

"*Kings*, Maggie?" Connor asked.

"Aye, kings is what they said."

David said, "I'm not surprised. This matter involves the English earl. Baines probably sent for King Edward. If he didn't, then King Alexander did. That tells me they want this issue ended."

Will smiled. "Well done, ladies. This is perfect. Our plan is already set."

———◆———

THEY SPREAD OUT AS SOON as they entered Edinburgh, not wanting to be noticed as a group. Now that her insides were no longer in a jumble, she noticed that what David had said was true. Unlike in the Highlands, where everyone proudly wore their plaid, almost half of the people she could see now wore no plaid. Gavin and Gregor were to conceal themselves in the trees, ready to fire their bows if necessary. Roddy and Braden were to stay just outside the gate, watching carefully to ensure no one of interest left without them noticing. Will and Maggie and Simone would huddle outside in disguise, while Connor and David would make their way inside to see Micheil Ramsay.

The latter group moved first, donning their plaids

declaring their clan affiliation before they approached the entrance to the castle. They spoke to the guards at the gate since David knew many of them.

"Who goes there?"

"David Drummond and my cousin, Alex Grant's son. What know you of my sire and mother? Are they still meeting with the king?"

"Aye. No one is allowed inside until they exit the meeting."

Maggie stood not far away, engulfed in a large cloak that hid both her and Simone. Will lurked in the shadows, waiting for a chance to move inside to the courtyard and blend in.

David began an animated story about a buxom wench that easily held the guard's interests, just the distraction Maggie and Simone needed. As soon as Connor gave her the signal, she opened her cloak and Simone darted out, rushing past the guards and into the gates to the royal castle. Maggie watched her run circles around the guards, who barely noticed her until it was too late.

At the same time, a low whistle carried across the courtyard. Will had called his falcons closer, causing many guards to glance at the sky, searching for the source of the flapping wings overhead.

The lassie made her way to the doors before she was stopped. Two guards held her up and she immediately started her story. The other guards ran over, so distracted by Simone's unexpected entrance they paid little attention to the rest of them. David continued to distract the gate guards while the falcons swooped closer, and Maggie was able to slip inside the castle gates, Will right behind her.

Simone, still disguised as a boy, continued her rant. "I'm the Earl of Wingate's messenger. I have an important message for him from Captain Granville. Take your hands off me."

Maggie had sidled up close enough to hear them, well

hidden behind a random jut of stone. She'd lost sight of Will, but she trusted he was hidden as well. One guard finally said, "Allow the lad inside. What harm could he do? He probably works for Baines."

The two guards let her down and one of them escorted her inside. The bulk of the castle guards were chatting with one another in the center of the large courtyard, and none of them noticed Maggie as she made her way over to an unguarded side door.

In the dark, it was even easier to slip about unnoticed. She made her way down the passageway and found an alcove to hide in close enough to the king's solar to over-hear the conversation.

She could hear the guard talking to the king at the door. "My king, this lad says he works for Baines and has an important message from Captain Granville."

"Fine," King Alexander said. "Out with it, lad."

She didn't hear anything from Baines, but Simone's voice come out in a rush, tremulous yet strong, just as they'd practiced.

"I don't have a message for him. I'm here to tell you Randall Baines tried to kill my sister. He left her to die in his castle and then tried to sell two lassies on the firth and he's a mean, mean man. I know because I used to work in his…" A roar of pure anger cut off her rambling speech.

"Who the hell are you? Shut her up. She's lying, my king. I'll whip your insolence out of you until you can no longer speak, you…"

A voice Maggie didn't recognize said, "How do I know she's lying, Baines? I've heard stories about you in England. We all have."

"He's lying. One of the Ramsays sent him, that bitch who…"

"Who what?" Her sire's voice rang out, followed immediately by her uncle's voice.

"How dare you speak of my niece in such a way."

"I wish to hear this again," King Alexander said. "Repeat what you said, lad. Wingate? Sit your arse down in the chair, and that's an order."

"The hell I will…I'll take care of that snit."

The next thing she heard was the pounding of Simone's feet as the lassie ran out the solar and dashed toward the door leading outside. Randall Baines followed, cursing oaths loud enough for all to hear.

Maggie smiled. Everything was happening at the pace they'd predicted it would. This was her chance. She chased Baines out the door and knocked him to the ground in the courtyard, flipping him onto his back and pouncing on him, a dagger pressed to this throat. "I think I'll wait until I have a full audience, my lord," she sneered.

"You again. I knew it, you bitch," he whispered. "I'll get the last laugh. My king is here this time."

"Silence!" she shouted.

A chaos of sounds erupted all around her, but she paid them no mind until King Alexander's voice rang out through the courtyard. "Hold your swords, all of you," he bellowed out.

Maggie could feel the sweat dripping between her breasts. She would finally get justice—for herself, for Molly, for Simone and Beatris, for Geva and Emma and wee lassies everywhere. She had the king's ear and she'd take full advantage of the situation.

King Alexander walked over until he was standing next to Maggie. "Let him go, lass."

She held her grip tight and her knee close to Baines's bollocks. "With all due respect, my king, not until he tells the truth. He's accusing me of things I didn't do, and I was imprisoned because of them."

The king bellowed, "Ramsay, get your daughter under control."

Aunt Diana came bustling over, her arms crossed in front of her. "That is my dear niece, and the man she has pinned to the ground did me a serious wrong many years ago, as I've been trying to tell you. I suggest you give her the chance to speak, Alexander. He wants you to hang her, does he not? Well, she is a loyal Scottish subject and she has the right to be heard."

Maggie began to tremble, but then she finally lifted her gaze to the courtyard. What she saw brought her strength. Simone stood beside Aunt Diana, holding her hand, and Maggie's uncle and sire were next to them. A man she'd never seen before stood behind the English guards, his hands clasped behind his back. Based on his royal robes, she guessed him to be King Edward. He said nothing, his gaze scanning everything in the area. Though five English guards had their swords pointed at Maggie, some of her cousins stood behind them, still dressed in black, swords out.

Her sire's voice carried to her as he whispered to his brother, "I question what my eyes are seeing, but I think we have a few nephews here, Micheil."

Uncle Micheil smirked. "Well, I'll be a horse's arse. Look at them all…"

King Alexander, who must have been directly behind them, said, "You'll be explaining this all to me later, Ramsays. Both of you."

Her sire spoke up the way he often did, loud enough to be heard in the Highlands. His booming voice almost brought a smile to her face. How she loved him, Gavin, and all her cousins who were here to support her. "My king, she is my daughter, and I ask you to allow her to speak. She deserves that much for all my clan has done for you over the years. I ask this boon."

While Alexander pursed his lips in silence, making his decision, Will stepped out of the shadows. His gaze caught hers, giving her the strength she needed to see this through. This wasn't just for the lassies, but for Will, for them. They both deserved their freedom.

King Alexander sighed. "Go ahead, lass."

"You're out of your mind, Alexander," King Edward said, shaking his head.

King Alexander chuckled, "Why? Someone neither of us trusts has accused her of great wrongs. Why should she not speak for herself?"

"But she's a lass…" Edward said.

"What in the hell does that mean?" Aunt Diana roared.

Maggie did her best to calm her racing pulse *and* her fury, thinking of Will and how much she loved him. This could be their only chance. She squeezed the knife against Baines's throat and said, "Tell them the truth. Tell him none of the people I injured at Wingate died from my wounds. Tell him your people were beating a lass of ten summers in front of the entire town for dropping something."

"She's not wrong there, Alexander," King Edward said with a nod. "I heard whispers, so I stopped at Wingate on my way here. Two of his guards are cursing and hobbling and the woman cussed a litany of oaths I haven't heard in a long time, but they're all quite alive."

Part of the truth had been outed, which made it easier to press for the rest. The kings both had to know. It was so wrong, so evil. Baines had to be stopped…and punished.

"Tell him about the lasses. Tell him how you wished to sell them and had to leave one to die. Tell them how you left a lass of five summers in her own filth to die alone." She did her best to hold her tears but a few escaped.

He didn't say a word, so she slid her knee closer to his bollocks.

Baines flinched. "Yes, I tried to make a little extra coin. I deserve it for how hard I work and my liege doesn't value me enough." With that last comment, he shot a glare at his king. "Three girls I wished to sell. That was it. Do you know how many children are sold every fortnight? There's an entire network of men who run the trade out of Edinburgh and London. They pay good coin to bring abandoned youths to those who want them, who adopt them, who don't have children of their own to love..."

"Don't insult us by pretending you did any of this out of the good of your heart, Baines," Logan sneered. "You were selling them to be slaves. The three girls he tried to sell should be safely on Ramsay land by now. They will vouch for themselves if you're in doubt, though one of them is so near death she may struggle to speak."

"Well, Maggie Ramsay," King Alexander announced in his deep brogue, "it seems there is no longer a bounty on your head. Let him up and you are free to go. His king can decide what to do with him, but one thing is certain. Edward, keep him on English soil, would you? I've had enough dealings with this fool. I'll gift your Scottish castle to another."

Maggie released Baines and stood, allowing him to get to his feet. He glared at her and made his way to King Edward's side.

King Alexander spun on his heel to go back inside, motioning for the Ramsays to join him. Will reached for her, but something caught her out of the corner of her eye. Will must have noticed the same because he reached for his dagger at the same time as Maggie.

CHAPTER TWENTY-THREE

RANDALL BAINES WAS RACING TOWARD King Alexander with his arms outstretched, a slow roar echoing out in the night. The dagger clutched in his hand looked wickedly sharp.

The fool was going to try to stab their king. Will could scarcely believe it, but there was no time to wonder at the man's stupidity. Only time to act.

Several guards saw it and yelled, taking action, but they were too slow. Maggie threw her dagger, catching Baines in the back of his neck. Will's dagger hit him on the left side of his back. Baines's forward motion stopped and the dagger in his hand clattered to the cobblestones in the courtyard. King Alexander heard the noise and spun on his heel, surprised to find Baines about to pounce on him— perhaps even more so to see he was instead falling to the ground with two daggers in him. Two arrows from the king's guards followed the daggers, catching him in the side and in his belly.

Pink foam reached his lips as he dropped to the ground.

Dead silence took over, the bystanders all stunned by the foolish earl's attempt to kill the Scottish king.

King Alexander's gaze traveled over his guards, then the English guards, then the intruders dressed in black, before returning to those standing closest to him. Finally, he asked, "Whose daggers are those?"

Will tugged Maggie to him, wrapping his arm around her. "Mine, my king," he said. He could not allow her to be imprisoned again.

Maggie glanced up at him as if she knew what he was doing. She said, "And mine."

King Alexander moved to stand in front of them. Will thought his heart would burst out of his chest, but he would not allow this man or anyone to take his wife from him. He pulled her closer, sweat dripping down the sides of his face and the back of his neck, wondering what would happen to them now.

"It seems I owe you both some thanks. What is your name, son?" he asked, glancing up at Will.

For a split second, he considered doing what he always did when asked for his name. He considered lying. But the time for lies had ended. He was done running, hiding from the world. He did not wish for his life with Maggie to be spent darting from shadow to shadow. She deserved more than that. "Will MacLerie, my king," he said without flinching.

"The same MacLerie who has been wanted for murder?"

Maggie peered up at him, tears misting her gaze as she shook her head ever so slightly. Later, if he was granted a leave, he'd have to help her understand why he'd acted so.

"Aye, the same, my king. I killed a man for burning my mother at the stake. He accused her of witchery after she saved the life of his nephew, and he made himself both judge and executioner."

King Alexander rocked back and forth on his feet, his arms crossed in front of him. "I've heard plenty of rumors about MacEwan's death, but even if you are guilty, you've just served your sentence by saving your king's life...as did this lass here. You are both free to go with my gratitude for your quick action."

Will shook his king's proffered hand, then kissed Maggie's forehead.

They were free.

Their king took a step back toward the castle before

turning around. "Actually, I'd like to speak to both of you in the presence of your sire, my dear."

Will glanced at Logan Ramsay and then at Maggie, both of whom looked as surprised by the request as he felt.

"See me inside in one hour, if you please."

———◆———

MAGGIE SAT IN A CHAIR in the royal solar, her husband on one side and her sire on the other. Will held her hand, though she had to pull away every few minutes to wipe the dampness from her palms onto her leggings.

Will said, "I don't mind. You need not do that. Mine are the same."

Her father got up and started to pace behind them, his steps echoing across the chamber. Simone had gone off to one of the royal chambers with Aunt Diana. In all likelihood, Micheil and her cousins were with them, enjoying a well-deserved meal.

They ignored her sire, listening to his footsteps as they continued their rhythmic back and forth movement.

Suddenly, they stopped. Something had surprised even her sire.

She pivoted her head in time to see both kings enter the back of the chamber, six guards following them. Alexander sat behind his desk while Edward stood off to his side.

"We have a proposition for you," King Alexander said.

Maggie didn't miss the arch of her father's eyebrow as he took the seat next to her.

King Edward said, "While Alexander will not ask, I will be blunt. MacLerie, are you the man known as the Wild Falconer?"

Will glanced at her and she gave him the briefest of nods. They needed to end all of the lies, all of the hiding, so they could live the lives they deserved.

"Aye, I have been called that, King Edward."

King Alexander didn't try to hide his smile. "How many

birds follow you, and how do you command them?"

"Only two, my king—a peregrine and a merlin that tend to travel together. They follow me at times, and they will assist me if I am in trouble."

No one said anything for a few moments. Maggie could feel her pulse speed up just because of the uncertainty. Why were they here in front of two kings?

The two great men exchanged a look, and then Alexander turned back toward them. "I'll put an end to this quickly. Edward and I are placing a royal request to you two. Logan, you've done me many favors, but 'tis time to use our youth. How much do you know about this network of criminals selling lassies? I know of the well-hidden movement of normal goods—whisky, wool, weaponry, but this? This is unspeakable. How old was the youngest lass who Baines tried to sell?"

"Five summers," Maggie replied. "There were two others, one is six and her sister is seven. This is the first we've learned of this atrocity."

King Alexander closed his eyes and pinched the bridge of his nose. "We must put an end to this."

His English contemporary nodded. "Agreed. You have my full support, but I'll allow you to handle this."

King Alexander glared at the other king for a moment, likely because of how he'd worded his agreement. "Our royal request is for you to do what you can to undercover this network of darkness. I know not what to call it at this point. I will finance your travels. 'Tis your choice if you choose to hire any assistance, but I don't want this to be general knowledge. You are to keep your true purpose hidden and report back to me once a moon. If you wish, you may have your sire or your uncle report to me instead, and I urge you to use their guidance when you require it. Hire only those you can trust to keep this quiet. What say you?"

Will squeezed her hand and she knew exactly what it meant. In unison, they both said, "Accepted."

Maggie added, "With pleasure."

———◆———

SEVERAL HOURS LATER, MAGGIE RAN up the stairs in the royal castle, eager to get back to her husband. She'd already said her goodbyes to her cousins and aunt and uncle. Uncle Micheil and Aunt Diana had left for Drummond land, while David had headed home with the Ramsays. To Maggie's delight, her sire had taken Simone under his wing.

King Alexander, however, had gifted Maggie and Will with a night in one of the castle's royal suites. Her husband had already gone up, and she couldn't wait to join him.

She stepped into the chamber, closing the door behind her, and gasped in shock at the size of the place. She spied Will at the far wall tending the fire in the hearth. He started to move toward her, but she held her hand up to him. "Nay, please do not move."

He gave her a puzzled look but did as she asked.

The chamber was twice as long as the largest chamber in the Ramsay Castle, so she decided to tease her husband a bit. She took one step toward him and asked, "Do you recall one of the first things you said to me when we traveled to Wingate together?"

He shook his head silently, his eyes taking her in. His gaze made her feel beautiful and not a little wanton.

"I do." She began to move toward him, a slow purposeful walk. With each step, she shed a piece of her clothing. "You said I would have to make the first move with you."

His chuckle amused her, putting a wide smile on her face.

"So I'm going to do that. You may not move, and you may not talk."

He broke into a wide grin and squared himself to her. Tugging his black tunic off, he tossed it aside and settled his hands on his hips.

She pulled her tunic off and dropped it to the floor. Her breasts were bound, so she unhooked the end of the linen wrap and pulled it over her head, then twirled about in a circle with each loosening of the wrap, pirouetting toward him. She was only a few steps away when her breasts broke free of their confinement.

His eyes dropped to them before flitting back up to hers, full of that smoldering look she loved. He removed his boots and dropped his breeches, standing boldly in front of her, his erection jutting out proudly toward her.

"Will, I wished to watch you grow. 'Tis no fun now." She removed her boots, her leggings, and her stockings, not stopping until she stood nude in front of him.

They stayed like that for a long moment, naked and silent, full of anticipation. Maggie's mouth went dry as she stared at her husband, taking in the broad expanse of his chest, the flat planes of his abdomen, the dark hair that covered his legs and covered him *there*. Hell, but the man was a tall beauty. She noticed the smirk in his expression, so she decided to tease him some more. Reaching up to cup her own breasts, she tweaked her nipples.

Her husband moved like a falcon, saying, "That was the wrong thing to do if you wished for me not to touch you." He lifted her up and pinned her against the wall next to the hearth, sliding his cock inside her with one thrust. She squealed with delight and moaned when he filled her completely, her slick juices making his every movement an exquisite torture.

He held her in his arms as she whimpered with pleasure, on the verge of something grand, and he finished with a few more quick thrusts. As he roared her name with satisfaction, she succumbed to his sweet torture, her orgasm coursing through her as he finished.

With a panting breath, she wrapped her arms around his neck and said, "That was fine and wonderful, husband, but you will take me to that royal bed and do the same thing before I leave this chamber. I wish to wallow in those pillows."

He laughed and carried her over to the bed, dropping her into the middle of the luxurious coverings before lowering himself over her body. "Your wish is my command, my lady."

———◆———

THREE DAYS LATER, MAGGIE SAT beside her sleeping sister, kneading her hands as she waited for Molly to wake up. So much had happened, but she needed to speak with her sister alone before she introduced her to Will. A crowd of people were celebrating their success and return in the great hall, but Maggie needed to do this before she could enjoy the festivities.

As soon as she opened her eyes, Molly screamed, "Maggie!" She sat up in bed, albeit a bit slowly, and held her arms open for her sister. There was not the slightest bit of anger or recrimination on her face.

Maggie fell into her sister's arms sobbing, beyond happy to see her smiling. "I'm so sorry for all the trouble I've caused you. Are you well?"

Molly tugged her down to sit on the bed beside her. The two of them plumped up a couple of pillows so Molly could settle back without putting too much pressure on her ribs. "Maggie, why do you think you've caused me trouble? My silly accident had naught to do with you."

"I heard Tormod found the person who shot at you?"

"Aye, 'twas a reiver who mistook me for a deer. Tormod gave him a bit of a beating, but then he sent him on his way. He told my husband 'twas an accident. Enough about me. Tell me all about you. So much has happened. You're married, aye?"

"Well, handfasted. Will MacLerie. He's a friend of Gavin and Gregor's."

Molly interrupted her, a huge smile on her face. "Tell

me the truth. Is he the Wild Falconer? Does he travel with birds?"

Maggie rolled her eyes. "Aye, he is, but he says most of the tales are false."

"But the falcons?"

"True, he has two of them. They are fine birds."

"Oh Maggie. I'm so excited for you and I cannot wait to meet him."

"I love him so much, but I'll let him tell you all about his past. He makes me so happy, Mol. But I must apologize for my part in your arrest."

"Papa was so angry with you in Edinburgh. The king already said he wouldn't try me because I've worked for the Crown for so long. He was just doing it to make Baines happy, hoping he'd go away. But then they locked you up. How did you get out?"

"Will. He helped me, and Gavin and Gregor and David."

"David?"

"Aye, Uncle Micheil and Aunt Diana heard all about it and got involved, but you'll hear the whole story below-stairs…if you're feeling up to it. Will you come down to meet Will?"

"Of course. But first we need to talk more about why you risked so much to protect me. Mayhap I cried about Baines while I was ill, but the man would never have bothered us again. I understand why you went after him, he was a blight on England, but you cannot risk your own safety like this. Maggie, be more thoughtful about what you do. I don't wish to ever lose you."

"I understand. 'Tis how I feel about you, but Will was with me most of the time."

"I'm glad you're married. You'll be less likely to run off alone again. Papa says you have a purpose? He would not tell me more."

"We'll wait for that. Will and I will explain it together. There's something else I wish to discuss with you." She paused, thinking on the one thing she had not yet told Molly. "Molly," she finally said, "part of the reason I left is because you were the only person who ever stood up for me. The only one who loved me. 'Twasn't because of you that Mama sent me to work for Baines. She didn't like me…" She was so ashamed that her own mother had despised her, she couldn't even finish the sentence, instead dropping her gaze to the floor.

"What are you talking about? Mama loved you. In fact, she was protecting you. That's why she sent you with me."

"Nay, I overheard her arguing with Papa one night before we left," she said softly, forcing the words out. "I heard her say she didn't like the way he looked at me. She sent me away because I was Papa's favorite. Because I was too pretty."

"Nay, 'tis not how it was at all," Molly insisted, leaning forward in her eagerness to speak. "Mama said she feared Papa would be inappropriate with you. Do you remember what Baines did to me? She feared the same for you, but with Papa or our older brothers. She told me she was sending you away to protect you. She feared Papa would…well, you can imagine the rest."

Maggie couldn't move, her heart pounding so hard in her chest. Was Molly right? Could it be true that her mother had truly loved her?

"Sister, 'tis true. Mama wanted you safe. She thought being in the earl's home would protect us. She had no way of knowing it would be dangerous."

Her mother *had* loved her. The knowledge unlocked something inside her, and the old hurt, which she'd carried around all these years, finally began to fall away.

"You need to stop trying to protect me," Molly said. "In fact, I'm going to direct your protection to someone else."

She had no idea what her sister was talking about. She could hardly hear her words because her mind was in such turmoil—a good kind of turmoil. "What? You mean Simone and Beatris and the other lassies? I'll do aught I can to protect them."

"Them, too, but not just them. I'm carrying, Maggie. You're going to be an auntie in about five moons. 'Tis why I've stayed in bed so much with my ribs. Aunt Brenna is worried for the bairn. But she thinks the worst is past, and I am feeling so much better. But I won't be working for the Crown again until some time after the bairn is born."

Maggie wished to jump for joy. "Molly, 'tis the most wonderful news I've ever heard!" She hugged her sister. "Is your belly rounding?"

Molly pulled her night rail up to show her, smiling with pride. "A wee bit, I think."

"Oh my, 'tis bigger. I'm so happy for you."

"And you will stop protecting me?"

"Well, you are carrying…"

"All right, but once the bairn arrives, you must start protecting the wee lad or lassie, not me."

"Agreed." She hugged her sister again. "May I tell everyone?"

"Most everyone found out while you were away. They promised they'd allow me to tell you myself. But I'd love to hear all about your adventure and meet your husband. Will you help me?"

"Of course." She helped Molly wash up and get dressed, all the time chattering about the wee lassies, who had already introduced themselves to her sister. She couldn't wait to tell Will he was going to be an uncle.

———◆———

WILL HAD NEVER MET SO many people before in one day. He'd had a difficult enough time remembering Maggie's band of cousins, as his grandpapa had called them. Now he'd met even more. And yet they were all kind, all accepting. He sat on the floor playing with Angus, hanging on to one end of a small section of rope while the wee puppy did his best to wrestle it out of his hand. There was no shortage of dogs here, though most were kept outside or in a small area at the end of the hall.

A few moments later, Maggie came down the stairs ahead of her sister, who looked much better than she had that day in Edinburgh. While their hair was different, the two had the same exact smile. With each step, Maggie glanced over her shoulder, her eyes full of worry and love, making certain Molly was safe. He sent Angus off to play with the other pups, then made his way to the bottom of the stairs to greet his wife and introduce himself to his new sister-in-law.

"I'm so pleased to hear you are married," Molly said with a big grin after the introduction had been made. "Maggie will make you verra happy. She has the biggest heart of anyone I know."

"I cannot argue that point." He wrapped his arm around Maggie's side, pleased to have her with him again. Part of him had worried she might change her mind about him once they returned to her family's keep, but he'd been foolish to worry.

Someone clapped their hands to get everyone's attention, so he found seats for the two sisters and stood behind Maggie with his hands on her shoulders. Logan stood in the middle of the hall, his hand raised to quiet everyone.

"I just wanted to say how proud I am of our daughter and her new husband, and of every last member of the band of cousins, as they've named themselves. I have to say I was stunned to see our young ones join together to handle this situation and exact vengeance on someone who has done this family plenty of wrong. Simone, you were wonderful. Everyone else, my congratulations, but especially to Maggie and Will, who saved King Alexander's life." Everyone began to chatter at once, so he held up his hand again. "I'll let the ones who were there tell their tale, but I also wish to welcome these four young lassies to

Clan Ramsay." He pointed to where the lassies were seated happily in a row. "We're most grateful to have you join us. I'll not talk any longer. Enjoy the food and each other. We have a wonderful clan."

Maggie's mother made her way over and sat across from them at the table. Maggie had greeted her quickly and introduced her to Will, but she'd been in a rush to get to her sister. There hadn't been much of a chance to talk. "I heard you put on quite a show, daughter. Well done. You handled yourself well, I hear. I also wish to let you know how proud I am of how you saved those lasses. We've made a decision about who'll take care of them. If you agree, your sire and I will adopt Simone and Beatris, and Geva and Emma will join Aunt Brenna and Uncle Quade's family."

"Many thanks, Mama. I'd love to consider Beatris and Simone my sisters." As if on cue, Beatris crossed the hall and climbed up onto the bench next to her new mother. She smiled at everyone before resting her head on Gwyneth's lap and falling fast asleep. "She's doing much better, but Aunt Brenna said she was in such bad shape that 'twill take her a while to catch up."

Her sire came over to join them and only said two words, "Married yet?"

"Papa, we handfasted, I told you that."

"You could have a big wedding if you wish," Gwyneth said.

She glanced up at Will to see if he had strong feelings either way, but he just shrugged. He didn't care what they did. This was up to Maggie. He was surprised to hear her response.

"Nay, Mama. I feel we're already married. We'll just visit Father Rab before we leave to make it official and to make Papa happy."

He leaned over and whispered, "I agree. You've been mine since we handfasted and naught will break us apart.

That is what I celebrate, not standing in front of a priest."
He held her heart just as she did his. They would be
together forever, and nothing would ever change that.

Her father made a growling sound, but then followed it
up with a grin. "I can't say aught bad about your husband,
Maggie. He did a fine job protecting you." Then he glared
at Will. "Make sure you *always* protect her."

"Before you leave?" Molly asked. "Where are you going?"

Maggie reached for her husband's hand lacing her fingers with his. "We've received a royal request to see if we
can uncover more of that network, the one that's selling
the lassies. We've accepted. The verra thought of it makes
me ill."

"Your actions are honorable, but please be careful," her
mother said.

"We will. With Will by my side, we'll be fine."

Will couldn't have said it better himself.

EPILOGUE

———————

A SENNIGHT LATER, WILL AND MAGGIE settled their satchels on their horses' saddles. They were taking two horses because she'd insisted on bringing a few more clothes this time. They were about to leave when they found themselves surrounded.

Will glanced at her brother and cousins, wondering what this was about. They hadn't confided in any of them yet about their task. David finally spoke, "We've decided we'd like to go after that network Baines was mixed up in. Are either of you interested?"

Will quirked his brow, glancing at Maggie to see what her reaction would be.

Maggie smiled. "All of you? Even you Grants?"

"Aye," Connor said. "We'll just need a little more time before we can get started. We must get word to our families."

Braden said, "If you'll join us, we thought to search out a deserted cottage, see if we can make it a gathering place of sorts. A place where we can sleep, if necessary, and meet to make plans."

Will and Maggie glanced at each other, and she nodded to him. Will said, "Go ahead. We'll need assistance, and who can we trust better than them?"

Maggie filled them in on their royal bequest, and her brother excitedly said, "Aye. We'll help you," before she ever asked.

She added, "But you must keep our purpose a secret."

They each heartily agreed.

Will said, "I think 'twould be wise for us to have a private meeting place. My grandsire would be pleased to have us. He's isolated and there are many hiding places on his land, but he doesn't have the extra room."

"Then mayhap we can build a cottage near him. We could help him while we're there, hunt for him. What say you?" Connor asked.

"Sounds wonderful to me. I know my grandsire could use the extra help." And he'd noticed how much the older man loved having young people around him. He seemed more invigorated now than he had been since Will's mother's death.

"I would welcome all of your help. I fear we may find more than we expect, and it could be more than the two of us could handle."

David said, "Whatever you find, we're willing to help. Let's clear Scotland and England of this plague."

"I think we need a name like Will had," Gavin added, waggling his eyebrows. "'Twill give us a reputation in the Highlands. Any ideas?"

"My grandfather said it best," Will said. "We're the Band of Cousins."

THE END

RAMSAYS

FAMILY TREE (1280s)

———

QUADE RAMSAY and wife, BRENNA GRANT
Torrian (Quade's son from his first marriage) and wife,
Heather—Nellie (Heather's daughter from a previous
relationship) and son, Lachlan
Lily (Quade's daughter from his first marriage) and husband, Kyle—twin daughters, Lise and Liliana
Bethia and husband, Donnan
Gregor
Jennet

LOGAN RAMSAY and wife, GWYNETH
Molly (adopted) and husband, Tormod
Maggie (adopted)
Sorcha and husband, Cailean
Gavin
Brigid

MICHEIL RAMSAY and wife, DIANA
David
Daniel

AVELINA RAMSAY and DREW MENZIE
Elyse
Tad
Tomag
Maitland

Novels by

Keira Montclair

———◆———

THE BAND OF COUSINS
HIGHLAND VENGEANCE

THE CLAN GRANT SERIES
#1- RESCUED BY A HIGHLANDER-
Alex and Maddie
#2- HEALING A HIGHLANDER'S HEART-
Brenna and Quade
#3- LOVE LETTERS FROM LARGS-
Brodie and Celestina
#4-JOURNEY TO THE HIGHLANDS-
Robbie and Caralyn
#5-HIGHLAND SPARKS-
Logan and Gwyneth
#6-MY DESPERATE HIGHLANDER-
Micheil and Diana
#7-THE BRIGHTEST STAR IN
THE HIGHLANDS-
Jennie and Aedan
#8- HIGHLAND HARMONY-
Avelina and Drew

Dear readers,

Thank you for reading *Highland Vengeance,* my first novel in my new series, The Band of Cousins. I do have several other novels planned for these characters, starting with David's story and ending with Connor's. Stay tuned for at least three more of these adventures in 2018.

As always, reviews would be greatly appreciated. Sign up for my newsletter on my website at *www.keiramontclair.com.* I send newsletters out with each new release.

Happy reading!

Keira Montclair

www.keiramontclair.com
www.facebook.com/KeiraMontclair/
www.pinterest.com/KeiraMontclair/

ABOUT THE AUTHOR

KEIRA MONTCLAIR is the pen name of an author who lives in Florida with her husband. She loves to write fast-paced, emotional romance, especially with children as secondary characters in her stories.

She has worked as a registered nurse in pediatrics and recovery room nursing. Teaching is another of her loves, and she has taught both high school mathematics and practical nursing.

Now she loves to spend her time writing, but there isn't enough time to write everything she wants! Her Highlander Clan Grant series, comprising of eight standalone novels, is a reader favorite. Her third series, The Highland Clan, set twenty years after the Clan Grant series, focuses on the Grant/Ramsay descendants. She also has a contemporary series set in The Finger Lakes of Western New York and a paranormal historical series, The Soulmate Chronicles.

Contact her through her website, *www.keiramontclair.com.*

www.ingramcontent.com/pod-product-compliance
Lightning Source LLC
Chambersburg PA
CBHW061134200626
46817CB00016B/1394